SOLDIER DOG

SAM ANGUS

SQUARE
FISH

FEIWEL AND FRIENDS
NEW YORK

SQUARE FISH

An Imprint of Macmillan
175 Fifth Avenue
New York, NY 10010
mackids.com

Square Fish and the Square Fish logo are trademarks of Macmillan and
are used by Feiwel & Friends under license from Macmillan.

Square Fish books may be purchased for business or promotional use.
For information on bulk purchases, please contact the Macmillan Corporate
and Premium Sales Department at (800) 221-7945 x5442 or by e-mail
at specialmarkets@macmillan.com.

A CIP catalogue record for this book is available
ISBN 978-1-250-04417-4 (paperback) / 978-1-250-03764-0 (ebook)

Originally published in Great Britain by Macmillan's Children's Books,
a division of Macmillan Publishers Limited
Originally published in the United States by Feiwel & Friends
First Square Fish Edition: 2014
Square Fish logo designed by Filomena Tuosto

11 10 9 8 7 6 5 4 3 2

AR: 6.0 / LEXILE: 870L

For Cary

PART I

13 May 1917

Lancashire

Twelve hours had passed. He'd last seen her at eight that morning. Faint with exhaustion and hunger, Stanley sank down. How on earth could he find a creature lighter and quieter than the wind? He called out to her but his voice was caught up and whisked away over the sedge grass. All day out searching he'd seen only five dogs. There were fewer dogs in Longridge now, just as there was less of everything, because of the War.

He rose and pushed his bicycle up, on beneath the tracery of a rowan, dizzyingly suffused and glowing with tarnished orange, on upward to Rocky Brow. Stanley called out again. A merlin rose and dashed away in alarm, but the sedge and the hawthorn gave no answer. Rocky Brow was Stanley's last hope. He'd said to himself he'd go all the way there and then turn back. When he got home, it would all depend on Da's mood. Stanley never knew what to expect anymore. Living with Da was like living with a volcano.

As Stanley approached the brow, a magnificent hound, his head and neck strong enough to hold a stag, appeared from the other side and paused on the crest, his feathered hocks whipping like banners in the wind.

"Where is she? Where is Rocket?" The dog, a deer-hound cross perhaps, lifted his handsome head, looking down, beyond Stanley, on the land below as though he owned it. Stanley raised his head too. "Hey, boy, where's Rocket?"

The warrior dog responded with a defiant stare, then loped easily away in the direction of Gibbon. They bred cross-dogs, deerhound mixed with collie, at Gibbon, and that was Jake, the crack Laxton sire. Da didn't think much of the Laxtons—tinkers he called them, both them and their half-breed dogs—poachers, in his eyes.

Stanley closed his eyes and bit his lip. He'd looked everywhere. There were only three roads out of Longridge and he'd cycled three miles out on each of them, calling and calling to Rocket. Everyone in the village had said they'd look out for her, they all knew Rocket. She'd be stolen, someone had said, a dog that valuable, but she wouldn't be stolen, she was too fast for that. She'd come home, sooner or later, but until she did, Stanley had to face Da. He rocked himself, racked with guilt, remembering Rocket with the sash draped over her the last time she'd won the Waterloo Cup. Over a three-day knock-out competition, she'd beaten sixty-three dogs to the greatest prize a greyhound could win. He saw Da and Ma and Tom and himself, the crowd of thousands, and the tears in Da's eyes as he held the glinting cup and chain.

"And don't come back till she's found." That's what Da had said. He couldn't have meant it, couldn't have meant Stanley to stay out all night. Miss Bird, his form teacher, had seen Stanley crossing and criss-crossing Longridge. The third time he'd passed her, she'd stopped him, and when he'd explained she'd said that of course Da would want him home, hadn't meant what he'd said, that Rocket would come home of her own accord, that she could look after herself. Wearily Stanley rose and turned for home.

By the empty gatehouse, he turned off the lane and passed beneath the gloomy spruce that clung to Thornley's north drive and the new lake. What should he say to Da? What would Tom say? This would never have happened to Tom. His brother would have known not to let Rocket out while she was still in heat. Stanley winced; it was all his own fault, he shouldn't have let her out.

Stanley paused at the arched entrance to the yard. He took a deep breath, squared his shoulders, and turned the corner.

Across the yard, next to the iron bars of the kennels, stood Da, hunched, dangerous, and explosive, white hair bristling, fists swivelling in his pockets. At his feet was Rocket's bowl, put out for her as always on the dot of five. How long had Da been standing there? Stanley gathered his courage and brushed his hair clear of his forehead.

"I c-can't find . . ." His throat was prickling, his words shrivelling in his mouth. "She'll c-come back . . ." If only Da would say something, look at him even.

Da's feet shifted, his shoulders collapsed, and he tramped toward the cottage. Stanley abandoned his bicycle and followed. There was Da, already slumped in his chair, scowling into the unlit hearth. He looked so old. Da was the husk of a man, a man shrunken and emptied by grief. That hair had once been chestnut, like Stanley's own, before sorrow turned it white, before Mother died, but Da wasn't that old, or at any rate, he wasn't as old as he looked.

Da's hands fretted the edges of his green cardigan as he stared at the photographs of Tom and of Mother on the mantel. Da only ever thought about Da and about Tom. There was Tom in uniform, looking smart and brave, on his collar the red rose of the East Lancashires. Tom always had that smile in his eyes. To his right, in a separate frame, was Mother. They both had the same sandy hair, hazel eyes, and steady gaze. There were six years between Stanley and Tom, Stanley was nearly fourteen to Tom's twenty. Since Mother had died, Tom had been brother, friend, and father to him. Then the day he'd turned seventeen, he'd enlisted and he'd come home, and with one hand on each of his brother's shoulders, he'd said, "I'm off, Stanley. Tomorrow. Look after our da. And I'll come back for you."

Da had at first grown silent. Then his grief turned to anger, his long, menacing silences interrupted by sudden violent rages as his love for Stanley changed to indifference, then to wounding scorn.

Stanley would remember the golden afternoons when he and Tom and Da had lain like hares in folds of soft brown grass as Da taught them to make reed whistles and sound the song of the curlew. They'd all been together that last afternoon before Ma's sudden death, sun-warmed and smiling, and Stanley had never imagined that all he'd thought so safe, so permanent, could fall apart.

A sudden shudder rattled Da's body and Stanley saw him pull his cardigan tighter around himself. Stanley sat at the table, still watching Da, waiting for a moment that might be less dangerous than any other. He took a deep breath and willed his words to come out whole, not splinter in his throat.

"Do you . . ."

Da's glare was turning, like the slow hand of a clock, across the room to fix on him. Stanley faltered and withdrew. Da exploded in a violent rush from his chair and launched himself at the mantel. He lunged at Rocket's silver trophy and spun around to the table, sending the ceiling light swinging wildly to and fro as he pushed the great cup into Stanley's face. Da jerked it forward again, forcing Stanley's head back.

"Aye, she'll be back. But never the same again." Da's hair stood in fierce tufts, his brows twitched like malevolent centipedes. He slammed the immense trophy down. "A bitch never runs so fast after whelping." Da rammed the iron bolt across the door and headed for the stairs.

Stanley looked through smarting eyes at the bolt. That door had never, ever been locked at night. Stanley took Tom's coat from the peg. He'd curl up in Mother's chair, with Tom's coat over him, so he'd hear Rocket if she pawed the door. If she didn't come during the night, he'd leave first thing tomorrow and go to the Laxtons at Gibbon.

Through the window, Stanley saw the empty yard, the chalked slots beside each box: Goliath, Milcroft, Warrior, Murphy. Those prized pure-blood horses Da had bred and broken in, every one of them gone. The yard had once been full, a dark-eyed head at each door. Da had been proud and busy, revered across the county for his shining, fine-skinned horses. Horses with bloodlines, he used to say, as pure as gods. How those horses had loved Da. How he'd loved them. Then each and every Thornley horse, twenty-three in all, had been requisitioned by the War Office. Only Trumpet, the old cob, was left.

It was a fine thing for a horse to go to war—that was what the master, Lord Chorley had said—a fine thing for a horse to serve in a glorious cause, in the war to end all wars, and anyway, they'd be back by Christmas. But it was May 1917 now and the War To End All Wars still raged.

Stanley huddled into the chair. After a while he slept and in his dreams he saw flocks of velvety puppies swarming and tumbling over shining cups, saw Da's gloom lifting and floating away.

A whoosh of icy air woke Stanley. The door was open—Da outside, grim and grey as a standing stone, Rocket's bowl in his hand. On paws light as raindrops, Rocket furled and unfurled herself around his legs. Stanley stepped forward.

"Da, she's b-back, she's h-here and she's all right, isn't—"

Da spun around with breathtaking speed.

"Some farm dog's been at 'er. Half-breeds she'll be bringing us now. Gypsy dogs, thieving, mongrel dogs. No, no respectable family has one of them." Stanley stood rooted in the doorway, hand still outstretched to his father.

"We're a gamekeeping family and there'll be no tinkers' dogs round here." Da's right arm shot out. Rocket leaped aside, quivering as the china bowl slammed into the stone wall, shattering into brilliant white shards. Da turned and left.

Stanley knelt by Rocket and hugged her close. She licked the boy's face and nuzzled him.

"Tom said the war would end quickly," Stanley whispered, "and when he comes back, Da will be better . . . Tom promised he'd come soon . . ."

Rocket blinked and turned to gaze into the house after her master.

School felt safer than home, though there were only two other boys, Joe and Arthur, in Stanley's class, most having left the minute they'd turned fourteen, taking work far away in the city factories to help their families. Stanley had been surrounded by friends once, but they probably wouldn't come back, even when the War ended.

Miss Bird's were Stanley's favorite classes—Biology and Chemistry, but especially Biology. Today Stanley was tired. The bench was harder than usual and his neck hurt because of the night in the chair. Miss Bird was teaching the respiratory system in humans but what Stanley wanted to learn was the reproductive cycle in dogs.

Miss Bird loved Tom, Stanley was sure of that, sure that she was waiting for Tom to marry her. It was awkward being only half awake in Miss Bird's classes because, being Tom's brother, she watched Stanley so closely, but she was giving him an easier time today, perhaps because of yesterday's search for Rocket.

How soon would the extra weight show on Rocket? How long did puppies take to arrive? Stanley had so many questions. Nothing useful was ever taught at school. Miss Bird (Lara, as Tom called her) knew so many useful things—she knew that dogs couldn't see as far as humans, saw six times less detail, that they were color-blind to red and green. She knew they had better night vision, greater peripheral vision, that horses' ears could turn a hundred and eighty degrees— she knew almost as much about animals as Da, that's what Tom used to say. Miss Bird would know about whelping and weaning.

Everyone was rushing out, cramming on coats. Biology was the last class and Stanley would have to go home now. He was always last to leave, he thought, as he picked up each colored pencil from his desk, one by one. Miss Bird liked different colors for veins and arteries. Joe grinned as he passed Stanley's desk, holding up a pack of scuffed playing cards.

"Tomorrow, Stan? Break-time? You won't win again." Stanley nodded. He was lucky at cards, always beating Joe. Joe rammed on his cap and left. Stanley thought about Joe's home, the hot tea and warm kitchen. How would things be at Thornley?

A hand rested on Stanley's shoulder.

"Stanley, I found this in the library and thought it might come in useful. For Rocket. Just in case, that is." Miss Bird was smiling. "It tells you everything you need to know." She held out a book.

"She came home, Miss Bird, she's back now."

It was a funny thing, but when he spoke to Miss Bird his words didn't dry and stick like needles—they came out as he wanted them to.

"How was your father? Was it all right when you went home?"

Stanley looked down at his desk. Miss Bird squeezed his shoulder and said quietly, "Don't forget how much he's lost, Stanley. Give him time . . . He's lost so much. And he's scared. You'll understand when you're older. You see, when you're your age, you're not scared of anything." Miss Bird was slipping something into his satchel: a jar of honey. She often gave him honey, knew Stanley liked honey, knew that his ma used to keep bees too. "Don't forget how much he's lost," Miss Bird repeated.

Stanley wanted to answer but there was something in his throat, not the dry stickiness but a lump, which wouldn't let any words out unless tears came with them. If he waited till he got to the door, he'd have his back to Miss Bird and he'd say it then; he must tell her what hurt so much.

"He hasn't lost me—Da hasn't lost me, I'm still here."

Four weeks had passed since Rocket disappeared. Stanley's birthday had come and gone unmarked. Only Tom had remembered. On the thirtieth, he'd said on the card, he'd be back. That was eighteen days away. These three years had passed so slowly, thought Stanley as he cycled homeward. Da was growing worse, each lonely evening with him more strained and oppressive. When Tom came home, Stanley would talk to him about Da, ask for his help.

Stanley pedaled harder. He must hurry, needed to collect the rabbits from the traps he'd set. He didn't have much time, so today he'd just skin one and give it to her raw. Da never fed Rocket now. Since he'd smashed her bowl, that's more or less when he'd stopped, so in the mornings Stanley would leave early and, checking the direction of the wind, set his three traps where the gorse was patterned with the crisscrosses of rabbit runs, as Da had once taught him.

Rocket was waiting for him by the door to Stable Cottage. She'd be hungry. Stanley leaned his bicycle against the wall, unlatched the door gently, and pushed. It only had to open a sliver to see if Da was there. Stanley released his breath; the room was empty. He listened. The house was empty. He slipped in, took a knife from the kitchen drawer, and ran, Rocket at his heels, to the glasshouse.

It was warm there, and cozy and safe. Since Oaks, the last gardener, had joined up, Stanley maintained what he could on his own, but there was so much to do at this time of year. Lord Chorley had written from London just to keep up the vegetable garden and the cutting borders, but with the big house dark and shuttered and the Chorleys away it was thankless, pointless work.

Rocket reminded Stanley about her supper with a nuzzle. Stanley looked down and saw her new sturdiness, and remembered. It was Monday today. Every Monday he measured her girth with a piece of garden twine and knotted it. Three knots last week, today he'd tie the fourth. He kept Miss Bird's book, *A Layman's Guide to Mating, Whelping, and Rearing*, in the glasshouse to hide it from Da. It was propped against the window and he'd read as he worked.

Stanley tipped the chopped rabbit into a terra-cotta pot and watched Rocket eat, smiling to himself with a mixture of guilt and excitement. Rocket raised her head to the boy, tail swishing in gratitude for the rabbit. Stanley put his hands on her flanks, feeling them, then slipping the twine under her belly. He tied a knot. A small but definite increase in her girth. Stanley had already calculated the date. If Rocket were to have puppies, she'd have them between the eighth and the sixteenth of July. More days to count up to, the days till Rocket whelped and the days till Tom came home. Years could go by just counting down to the things Stanley wanted to happen.

"He won't mind . . . Da won't mind . . . not once he sees them. Once he sees them, he'll love them . . . I'll keep one for me, one for Tom—and Joe wants one . . ."

Rocket sat panting. She'd grown hungrier, sat more readily now, was more affectionate.

When the light ebbed and Stanley could no longer see, he stopped work. He'd go in and make himself a honey sandwich, then he'd do his homework.

As he approached the cottage, Stanley lowered a protective hand to Rocket's head. Da was in his chair, the back of his head to the window. Apprehensive, Stanley pulled a soft minky ear to and fro between his fingers, then his heart somersaulted—Da had a card in his hand. Was it from Tom? Why was Da not moving? What had happened? Was Tom all right? Stanley flung the door open.

"Da—"

Without rising or turning, Da grunted something incomprehensible. He tossed the card on to the table. Stanley vaulted forward and took it. "Souvenir from France" was embroidered on it in yellow beneath a bower of flags. Stanley read:

Messines, 10 June 1917
Dear Father, dear Brother,
I was granted a week's leave to come
home and had got as far as Calais
when they wired to call me back. We are
preparing for another big stunt so now
I'm only granted two days' leave in the
field. I'm so disappointed not to come
home. I miss you both and long to see
you. I wonder if you heard the explosion
at Messines — they say it was heard in
Downing Street.
           Your loving Tom

Stanley stared at the thick cream card, blinking fiercely. Tom wasn't coming home. He was all right, but he wasn't coming. Stanley breathed slowly in and out; he must be brave or Da would lash out.

When Stanley looked up, he saw that Rocket had slipped in too when he'd come in. She sat at Da's feet, and he was glaring at her sturdy belly, her dull coat. Rocket's nose was tilted upward toward Da. Though Da no longer fed her, though he'd turned from her, still she followed his every movement, still he was the sun around which her earth moved.

"Come the time, the tinkers' dogs'll go where they belong. Aye, the tinkers'll take 'em." Da had risen and was standing by the opened door, his face to the night, Rocket at his side, immediate as a shadow, tail quivering. "No one else'll have them, not with the Dog Tax set to rise again—from seven shillings and six to ten shillings it's due to rise, and who'll be paying that for bastard half-breeds?"

Da clamped the door shut behind him, grazing Rocket's nose. He always used to walk her at this time before putting her in the kennel for the night. Now he'd ignore her and wander out alone. Stanley looked at Rocket, hovering, nose to the crack of the door, keeping vigil for her master's return, and he blinked back the tears that rose. He knelt by Rocket, holding her, but his eyes strayed to the photograph on the mantel—Tom in his uniform, earning his own wage, free and far from here.

"Lucky Tom," he whispered to Rocket, smiling sadly and tousling her ears. "If it weren't for you"—he laid his head against her long neck—"if it weren't for you and your puppies, I'd go away too . . ."

10 July 1917

Lancashire

The days were still long and lovely, but after dark there was no escape from Da. He'd grown stiller and somehow more combustible. As Stanley did his homework at the table, Da sat with his back to his son, that hunched form radiating scorn.

Stanley finished his equations. He twirled his pencil, thinking. There'd been eight knots in the twine yesterday, the increases bigger now and Rocket restless, her eyes strange and dilated. Today she'd refused her food.

Later, Stanley lay on his bed. There was a good haul of moths around the ceiling light above him. July was a rich month for moths and it was a good, warm night. There were two heart-and-darts up there, plus a mottled rustic and a brown house moth. *Lacanobia thalassina*. He tongued its Latin name as he watched the house moth. He had a good head for Latin names, liked they way they sounded.

Stanley sighed and rolled over to face the magazine cuttings on his wall of Egyptian tomb carvings of greyhounds. The dogs were described in stone with a clarity and precision and economy that Stanley loved. Rocket was like that, as noble and ancient and perfect as the Egyptian tomb carvings. She'd once been, he thought guiltily, the perfect specimen, the perfect greyhound, descended in a pure line through three thousand years of history from the dogs of Pharaohs.

To the right was a postcard Tom had sent earlier in the year, of an ambulance dog. It was a rough-haired collie dog with white-tipped tail feathers and smart saddlebags with a large cross on them. She stood in profile to the camera. Tom always found special things to send. Without taking it down, Stanley could picture the neat hand squidged in right to the edges, below 'ON ACTIVE SERVICE', the military Field Post Office number and the one-shilling stamp. Looking at the collie, he mouthed the words he knew by heart:

Pas de Calais
13 April 1917

Dear Father, dear Brother,
I have been warned to return to the
trenches any minute now. They say the
big push will be soon and we're making
final preparations, but the waiting feels
long. We pass our spare time in climbing
to the top of a slagheap to watch the
firing at Vimy Ridge — about four miles
away. And I watch the horses being
trained to machine guns. They learn so
very fast to turn their heads aside. It
is odd and cruel that the cavalry use
horses to draw machine guns when there
are now great machines like tanks about.
I always look out for the Thornley
horses, Da, and I pray for them — the
conditions are terrible for horses. The

wine is four foot high and even after tanks have flattened it horses should never be made to cross it.

I thought you'd like this picture, Stanley, of the ambulance dog. Every time I see a dog, I think of you, and of Thornley and I long to be home. It should be soon, as they say the german will is close to breaking. I will always be thankful that you were too young to fight — the world will never be the same again for those of us here.

Your loving Tom

"I will always be thankful that you were too young to fight." Did Tom not think that Da could be dangerous too? A knot tightened in Stanley's belly. Too young to go to war but not too young to be left alone with Da.

There was a rap on the door. Stanley started and sat bolt upright, heart racing. Da never came into his room.

"She'll be about ready now." The words were mumbled. "The log shed'll happen to be warm and dry."

Stanley catapulted himself out of bed and flew down the

stairs, then turned and ran up again. Da was excited about the puppies, he would love them. He, like Stanley, must have been watching and waiting. From under the bed Stanley grabbed a small tin box, and as an afterthought, the jersey strewn across his chair. He hurled himself down the stairs, then turned and ran up again to snatch the towel hanging under the washbasin. Cotton, iodine, towel—did he have everything? He lost his footing on the narrow treads, saving himself with a clutch at the banister, stubbing a bare toe on the iron boot-pull.

He hobbled around to the shed and edged the door ajar. A lozenge of moonlight slipped through and rested on Rocket, who lay panting on a straw litter.

Stanley squatted on his heels, his bare feet on the stone floor, the lantern above him casting a warm glow. No light shone from the Hall or the cottage. Only the log shed was warm and light and alive. An occasional shiver rippled along Rocket's flank. Shreds of mist curled in, hugging the stone and dissolving in the cozy fug of the shed. Da had prepared this moonlit bed for Rocket. He'd known the right time, known where she'd want to be; Stanley, for all his book, thermometer, and twine, hadn't.

Tremors shuddered through Rocket, one after another in quick succession. Violent quaking overtook her. Her hindquarters convulsed. There was something there beneath the rigid tail, sheathed in a white cocoon—the crown of a tiny head. "Anterior presentation," the library book had called it, the right way for a puppy to come out. Rocket's body juddered again—it was out, its eyes and ears sealed shut, all perfect rosy paws and folded limbs. Rocket put herself to a vigorous, workmanlike licking. The tiny thing yelped and yelped again and it was breathing on its own. Rocket chewed its cord and nuzzled the pink-nosed, pink-bodied pup towards her. It squirmed closer on its belly and then it was suckling.

Rocket tensed again, her body in spasm, legs rigid. One more cocoon emerged—it was all happening so quickly. Rocket was licking and chewing and there it was, wriggling, sightless, toward a teat. Two minutes passed, then Rocket convulsed again and there was one more. Three healthy pups. Were any still to come? Rocket's tapering head, more slender even than her neck, rose and she looked at Stanley, bright and intent, her open jaws now tensing, now panting.

Still with wonder, chin cupped in his hands, Stanley gazed at the little nativity. Rocket's body made a wreath around her brood. The puppies, all bitches, jostled in this perfect crib, their mewings and cawings, a tiny choir.

Stanley longed for Da to come. He'd love them, he'd love their gypsy coats, their splodges of color like spilt paint, couldn't not.

A sudden movement from Rocket jolted him. Her legs were in spasm. Something was wrong—she needed help—there must be a puppy stuck in the birth canal. It could be fatal if she'd been straining too long—twenty minutes at least had passed since the last pup. Beneath her tail Stanley glimpsed a white sac and his heart stopped: he could see one tiny outstretched paw—one foot first was dangerous. Rocket's eyes were still intent on his and they were too brilliant, brilliant with fear. Should he run for Da? Would she be all right while he was away? He heard footsteps. Da had come. Somehow Da had known Rocket needed him.

Even in her distress, Rocket uncoiled herself in welcome, her jaws half open in a valiant smile.

"Tinkers' dogs. Thieving dogs, that's what they are."

Rocket's eyes never left Da, but the pistol whip of his tone made her smile grow hesitant.

"Quick, Da, something's wrong."

Da grunted. He made no move for a second, then grunted again and knelt. He leaned forward and with one finger inched the tiny limb back in. Da waited. Minutes passed. Rocket shivered, then as she contracted, Da pulled the towel from his son's knees, ready for her. This time there were two tiny paws, two tiny folded limbs, and between the tips of two fingers Da held them and began to pull with a hold so sure that he seemed not to be pulling at all. The drawing out of the puppy was imperceptible; the movement of Da's arms in an arc across the belly, toward Rocket's head, imperceptible.

There it was: a sightless, soundless bundle. Da laid it between Rocket's forepaws. Watching his father, a tentative smile formed on Stanley's lips. Da rose. His fists clenched and he turned his head away from Rocket's shining head. He shifted and stood hunched under the lintel, eclipsing the light, throwing Rocket into darkness.

"It'll never live . . ."

The puppy was there between Rocket's forelegs, but it lay still and silent and she'd made no move towards it. Stanley must do something. With a pounding heart he gathered it up and held it cupped in the palm of one hand. He rubbed it with a corner of the towel until the downy coat was clean.

It was greyish white from nose to tail, the only puppy to have no markings, and Rocket's only son.

Stanley heard a sort of snort from the shadows behind him and hesitated, stalled by the force of Da's scorn. Rocket lifted her snout, brows arched, dark eyes bright and questioning. The plain white pup lying in the palm of Stanley's hand was too still. Rocket nosed the palm that held it. He must do what Rocket trusted him to and save this puppy. He lowered it to his lap and with hurried, panicky fingers, pulled some cotton from his tin box and tied a knot around the cord. Feeling Rocket's eyes follow his every movement, he cut the cord on the far side of the knot and placed the pup beside Rocket. The others mewed and cawed and sucked, but the weak pup was still motionless, inert. Amid the strident mews and bleats, that tiny body was silent, lifeless.

Rocket nuzzled the puppy to separate him from the sibling scramble, to stir him to life. She licked and nosed him but after a little while, her head sank, disheartened.

A few seconds passed.

Again Rocket raised her head and nosed the weak one. Stanley's breath stopped as she opened her jaws and picked him up. Hampered by the freight of bodies tugging at her, she clawed her way to Stanley and placed the pup on his lap. Stanley hesitated. Rocket nudged the lifeless bundle closer, eyes intent on the boy's face.

Rocket was asking for help. Stanley's fingers began to move before his head knew what to do. He'd already lifted it to his ear. It wasn't breathing—there was no heartbeat. He must move fast—the book said blocked airways could cause this, that you had to act quickly. There was no time to be squeamish. Stanley raised the tiny pink nose to his face, joined his own mouth to the minute nostrils, and sucked. Nothing. He sucked again. That was it. Such a tiny amount you could hardly tell. He spat, then held the little body to his ear. Still nothing. He must get it breathing. With the pads of his thumbs, he rubbed it all over, rubbed again, then held the pink nose to his own mouth to suck again and as he did, it squirmed and cried.

Stanley held out Rocket's son in the cradle of his palm. Her tail rose and fell with soft slapping as she sniffed and licked and sniffed and licked. She looked up at Stanley and her jaws opened and the warmth in her eyes felt like sunlight to the boy.

"It'll never be any good. It'll never live unless you'll be giving it a bottle." Da kicked the door open. "All of 'em. Manky Gypsy dogs, all of 'em." His voice boomed. Stanley shivered in the rush of damp air, his toes and fists clenching. "No one'll take 'em. Only the tinkers'll have your manky half-breeds."

He tramped away. Rocket's head followed her master's steps, her tail faltering, then falling and lying still. The footsteps stopped. Da's voice blasted out as though to rattle and shiver the stars above. "If the Gypsies won't have 'em tha'll drown 'em."

24 July 1917

Lancashire

Stanley collected the child's bottle from the draining board and, casting an apprehensive look toward the door, filled it with Lactol. There'd been no more talk of drowning but he lived in fear of Da's threats. He fetched the white pup from the kennel. The extra vitamins were doing him good; the pup would survive, whatever Da said. Every day all of them were heavier, their eyes open now, their bodies still soft and helpless and sleepy. Stanley settled down at the table.

The front door banged open. Stanley started, lifted the pup to his chest. Da saw it and scowled. One of his lightning rages was about to strike. Stanley's arm tightened involuntarily around the puppy.

"I should've drowned 'em. They'll only end up shot. The police are out there collecting every mangy half-breed dog from every street in every city in the land, and do you know what they do? They shoot 'em. Bang."

Da's rage had collapsed as quickly as it had erupted but weeks had gone by and he hadn't spoken a word. His absences from the house had grown longer, and his silence somehow more malevolent.

The white pup was tugging at Rocket's blanket, trying to wrest it out of her basket, his unsteady legs skating and slipping on the worn slabs. That little tail would be long and feathery like a Laxton dog's. Stanley grinned, remembering the dog on Rocky Brow. It was a good thing Da didn't know the sire was a cross-bred dog. Stanley knelt. The pup abandoned the blanket, bounded forward, and hurled himself at Stanley. Stanley put his nose to the pup's and they kissed like Eskimos.

"It's your last day on Lactol." Stanley ran his fingers along the pup's belly, down his haunches. "Two weeks old. Too big for Lactol. Almost time to wean you."

"Soldier," Stanley whispered. "Soldier." He'd named all of them now. Bentley was to be Tom's dog. She had a rough white coat, speckled with flecks of tan and a tan saddle. Tom had always loved Lord Chorley's ivory automobile, the one with the tan leather trimmings. Tom would be so pleased when he saw her. Biscuit and Socks were both tricolored, with black upper coats and white socks. Biscuit had a tan eyepatch. Only Soldier had a coat the color of porridge, and eyes as dark and soft as sable. Soldier would be Stanley's own dog.

"Soldier," he whispered again. "Soldier, you're named for my brother Tom . . . He should have been home by now . . ."

Da appeared, sudden and glowering, lurching at Soldier, swinging him up by the scruff of his neck, his tiny legs rigid and jumbled together. Da marched to the door and tossed Soldier out on to the cobbles. Stanley gasped, but in an instant, Soldier was up, bewildered, skittering lopsided toward the kennels, tail tucked down, anxious eyes and head curved to the door. Da tramped across the room and up the stairs.

Stricken, Stanley went to the pup. "He doesn't mean it . . . Da's only trying to hurt me." Filled with flinty anger, Stanley grew defiant. "But I'll go, run away, go and find Tom." Stanley's words took root. Yes, he thought, kneeling and stroking the pup. Yes, I'll go away from here, then how will Da feel?

Soldier licked Stanley's cheeks and that tiny, solicitous tongue, troubled eyes, and milky breath put an end to all thoughts of leaving home.

21 August 1917

Lancashire

Outside all was grey midsummer mizzle, but Trumpet's box was golden and warm. Stanley was filling some hessian sacks he'd taken from the potato shed with straw to make the puppies' bedding plusher. Trumpet was harrumphing and tossing his head, displeased at so much commotion in his box.

Stanley watched entranced as Soldier skittered about, raising dust that glittered like confetti. Soldier feinted a crouch, sprang away, then crouched again, inviting Stanley to play. Rocket unraveled herself, legs stacked just so, a reclining empress surveying her mischievous troops with amused tolerance. Stanley stuffed a final handful of straw into the last sack. Tom said he slept on a palliasse, that the Army gave one to each man, and Soldier, too, would have a palliasse. Stanley pulled the string tight and knotted it, watching as a pup jumped up at Trumpet's feathered forelegs.

"Six weeks old today and you'll have rabbit for lunch. Your first rabbit meat."

Stanley stood and turned to Trumpet and blew into his large nostrils. Trumpet held his great head still. He liked it when Stanley did that. Stanley turned and unlatched the door of the box to fetch some water. His step faltered as he found himself face to face with Da.

"Put the 'orse in the harness."

Da's voice was a guillotine. Soldier grew tremulous, and cowered. Wary, watching Da, Stanley fetched the harness. Why wasn't Da in his Sunday best? Weren't they going to church? Eyes still on his da, Stanley fitted the harness.

"It's to Birdy Brow and the tinkers we'll be going the day with your half-breeds."

Stanley clenched his fists, flint flashing in his eyes.

"N-no, no!"

"You'll do as I'm telling you, you dolt. An' stop your gab-bing and sputtering. The tinkers'll take 'em and they can take them for nought if there's not a word said. I'll have no Gypsy dogs in our house."

Motionless with rage, frustration, and fear, Stanley's un-formed words dried in his throat.

"One hundred hounds shot last week. Hounds with thor-oughbred in their veins. A fifty percent reduction—aye, fifty percent—in the numbers of hunting dogs, is what's ordered. Breaking men's hearts as have tended and fed those pure-bred packs—built them up over generations and—bang!—horse meat for France. An' you're thinking to keep mangy, good-for-nothing half-breeds, when thoroughbreds are be-ing shot?"

Stanley looked at the pups, saw in a sickening rush how small they were, only two handspans high. Too, too early to take them from their mother. Da stepped forward and raised his arm.

"I'll clout you . . ."

Stanley turned away, his heart pounding, flashes of anger breaking over him in waves of molten lava.

He had no choice. If the pups went to the Gypsies, they would, at least, be safe, they wouldn't be drowned. He'd lose Soldier, but this would be the last time he'd obey Da. Ever. If Soldier was given away, if they were all given away, then Stanley would leave home.

Pulling his cap over his eyes, Stanley backed Trumpet up to the trap, and spread some matting down. He lifted a pup and placed it in the trap. Rocket circled, nose raised. Avoiding Rocket's eyes, Stanley gathered Socks and Biscuit, so small he could hold them both with one arm. Only Soldier still to find—there he was, beneath Rocket, tugging at her, struggling to keep up as she paced to and fro, her searching head straining up at the trap.

Stanley would have to pull Soldier apart from Rocket, to pull the son from the mother. Stanley bit his lip, braced himself, and knelt. Rocket placed her nose on his lap, her trusting eyes searching his face. Stanley looked away as he tugged Soldier, feeling the resistance as the pup pulled at the teat. He held Soldier's plush puppy coat to his cheek, smelling his milkiness, remembering the horror of losing a mother.

"I won't let them take you, I'll find a way," he whispered. Turning and rising, he fumbled his way to the back of the trap.

The trap joggled over the yard toward the arch.

Stanley gasped. There was Rocket trotting along beside them, questing snout reaching upward. Stanley winced—he should have locked her up, hadn't been thinking straight—of course she'd follow her pups. Da turned Trumpet to the left. He was taking the drive that curved across the park, the drive the Chorleys called Park Drive. Still Rocket kept pace with the trap, at an airy trot, her feather-light paws barely disturbing the glaze of drizzle on the ground. Stanley lifted his hand to her in a motion to stay, hissing, "Go back. Go back."

Trumpet lumbered onward, and still Rocket followed.

"Go back, girl," hissed Stanley again.

They'd left the park and were almost at the new lake. Desperate now, Stanley stood and motioned again. "Go back, Rocket, go back."

Da's head turned. He saw Rocket.

"Home. Go home, girl," he yelled.

Rocket stopped.

"Gerraway. Back! Go back, girl."

Da whipped the old horse onward. Rocket cringed and recoiled two reluctant paces. There was a crack as Da's whip lashed Trumpet's rump with shocking violence. The trap gathered speed. But there was Rocket again alongside, effortless and gossamer and lovely. Da lashed the ground inches from her nose. Rocket flinched, then followed, now at a hesitant, bewildered trot, tortured between her instinct for obedience and her anguish for her brood. Da turned to Stanley.

"Are you still gawpin'? I'll clout you too . . ."

The puppies skidded across the trap, drawn ever away from their mother by Trumpet's awkward, uneven canter. Da jerked his arm up as though to hurl a stone. Rocket recoiled, quivering. She stayed there, one foreleg lifted and poised. There by the edge of the lake, in the unnatural, deathless shade of the spruce, she stayed and raised her nose to the grey sky, and howled.

Trumpet labored up between the dry stone walls of Birdy Brow, then down between the humps of gorse where the ground was harder, the windswept thorns twisted and tortured.

They reached a simple stone bridge and joined a straight, Roman sort of track, known as the Ribble Way, running through tussocky grassland. Ahead lay the Bowland Hills. Boulders dotted the treeless bog, the colors of the shrub heath muted by the veil of mizzle. Above, outraged clouds scurried across the enormous sky.

The road began to climb. This was a long way for an old horse. Stanley strained to see through the mist and the drizzle—something was going on ahead; it was difficult to see what. They drew closer. Some sort of gathering.

Da pulled up on a saddle of land that had been concealed as they'd climbed from below. Several other traps stood about. Ponies were tethered close by. Rough-looking men milled around holding large dogs on short ropes. Each dog had a form similar to Rocket's, but with a different coat and marking, all greyhound crosses: lurchers.

Some men sat on straw bales, smoking pipes and watching. Others stood shouting and arguing around a roped enclosure with a loudspeaker and a hard board painted white with numbers on it. Da dismounted, leaned over the trap, and hissed, "Criminal dogs and criminal men." He gestured to the huddle of men around the white board. "Respectable men are at church on a Sunday, while the tinkers and the poachers are out and about with their thieving dogs."

Apart from the gathering, and away from the loudspeaker, sat the man Da had come to see. Stanley knew him by sight. A large, handsome man, Darkie Lee was a figure of local legend, said to be able to take a hare in its form with his bare hands.

"Keep your mouth shut," Da growled as they picked their way closer.

Lee wore a black felt hat and woollen tunic with the sleeves pushed up. His eyes were trained on some bacon on a neat kindling fire. Around him a herd of barefoot children ran pell-mell. To his left, sat an iron-grey, one-eyed, wolf-like dog. Something nasty had happened to that missing eye, a tear on barbed wire perhaps. Lee raised his cap, but not his head, nor his eyes. Da squatted, on the near side of the fire, to talk to Lee. The dog growled. That growl was a warning of his loyalty to Lee. It growled again. The dog couldn't see Da's eyes because of his cap, and dogs, Stanley knew, like to see a man's eyes. He stepped forward and lifted Da's cap off. Da gave an irritated shrug. Holding the cap, Stanley stepped back.

"That's right," Lee said. "A good dog's always suspicious of a hat if he doesn't know the man."

Beyond Lee, two lurchers, one brindled, one black, were straining at their collars. A team of beaters were driving a wild hare a hundred yards or so ahead of the dogs. The crowd tensed. The springs in the dogs' collars were released. The collars flew open and the dogs sprang forward, the hare zigzagging ahead with breakneck changes of direction.

With a sudden spring, the brindled lurcher seized its prey, and in seconds the race was over, the dog turning and trotting smoothly back, holding his leggy, long-eared prize. That dog, thought Stanley, that could be a Laxton dog if its coat were longer. Da coughed and grunted.

"Pups. Rocket's pups, but rough-coated. Some sort of cross."

Lee's hawk-like eyes returned to the fire and he flipped the bacon. He slurped tea from a tin mug, removed the bacon from the fire, emptied his mug, and rose, indicating Da's trap with the merest inclination of his head.

Stanley leaped up and ran to the trap—he must get there first and hide Soldier. He whistled and Soldier sprang up and scampered over to him. Before Da and Lee reached the trap, the wriggling Soldier was hidden in Stanley's coat.

Lee leaned his elbows on the trap and inspected the cargo. Soldier buried his snout in Stanley's armpit, snuffled furiously, then scrabbled to break free. Stanley squeezed him with his arm, willing him to be still. Lee adjusted his hat.

"You've brought 'em on good. Nice condition on their coats. Shining eyes." Lee's own roving, glittering eyes stopped on Stanley.

"Their dam ran twenty-one courses in good company, and led in eighteen on 'em." said Da.

A longer silence followed. There were the sounds of a fight breaking out somewhere among the straw bales.

"They're yours if you'll have 'em," Da said to Lee. He gestured to the pups in the trap, looked mystified for a split second, then glowered and swung around, ripped open Stanley's coat, yanked Soldier out, and hurled him into the trap. Lee moved his head neither to right nor left but his hooded eyes were hard and penetrating as they flickered to and fro.

Soldier bounded across the trap. Stanley's arms curled around him and Soldier sheltered there. Lee's eyes rested on Soldier.

"I'll not take the queer one."

"Nought wrong with 'im." Da bristled.

"Nought wrong, but they're always softer, the white ones. Aye, and a hare turns from a white dog faster than from any other." Stanley squeezed his arm around the puppy, brimming with hope—he might keep Soldier, might bring a pup back to Rocket.

Lee gave a discreet wink at Stanley.

More to himself than to anyone else, Da growled, "His dam won twice on the Withuns." He snatched Trumpet's reins, ready to climb up into the trap.

Lee smiled at Stanley, a disarming smile of sporadic gold teeth. Still watching Stanley, he whistled. A fierce, raven-haired girl materialized beside him. Stanley stared at her and at the catapult she held. She stared back, unimpressed. Lee lifted Bentley by the scruff of her neck and held her up—Tom's dog, that was to be Tom's dog.

"A good rough coat. That'll protect her from the wire on the fences."

Da winced—Lee used dogs for poaching; that was why he liked the rough coats.

"Eh, an' look at her tawny eye. A tawny eye's a sign of a good, hard dog." Lee handed Bentley to the catapult girl. He lifted Socks and Biscuit. Stanley saw Biscuit's tiny wet nose, the eyes live with terror, and felt sick; she was so small.

"They're only s-six weeks—"

"Aye, six weeks is grand."

Stanley looked at the catapult girl. She looked, he thought, as though she might stew puppies for dinner.

Da was sitting in the trap, glowering into the heather. Hugging Soldier, Stanley raised his collar against the sharp wind and climbed up. Lee adjusted his hat, putting an end to the business.

"Look after them," said Stanley.

Lee leaned over the back of the trap. Smiling his white and gold smile, he said, "If a dog loves you, he'll do anything for you." Da cracked the whip. The trap lurched away. Lee adjusted his hat once more and sauntered off, dangling the tiny pups from the scruff of their necks.

Rocket was waiting where Stanley last saw her, ears pinned against her skull, foreleg poised, her pitiful, expressive form reflected in the black lake. Trumpet lumbered on. Rocket sprang forward and tore around the trap in joyful hoops. Holding Soldier, Stanley jumped down. He knelt, opened his coat, and watched with prickling eyes as Rocket licked and nosed her son. She grew wary and still, her son trotting ecstatic circles around her, his porridge coat glowing in the deep shade, his tail a circling blur. Rocket paused her licking and nosing, looked up after the trap, sniffed the air, then dropped her tail and began again, wounded and watchful, to caress Soldier.

4 September 1917

Lancashire

The little pup followed to heel but that was only because of the brace of rabbit hanging from Stanley's left hand. Stanley reached the Park Drive gatehouse and hesitated. He preferred the farm drive, but Da might be there at the lake again and Stanley had something he was looking forward to giving him. From his coat pocket, Stanley took a reed whistle.

"This is to train you," he said to the pup. "And to bring you to heel . . . and to make you sit." He blew. "This is for when you are ready to be trained."

Up on the moor, Stanley had cut two, one for himself and one for Da. He'd made them the way Da had taught both him and Tom. Da might help to train Soldier, the way he'd once trained Rocket.

They reached the lake. Da was there, hunched beneath the rigid spruce, Rocket a few feet away. How long had Da been there? Why?

"D-Da . . . L-look, I've made you a whistle . . . to train Soldier . . ."

Da didn't turn at his son's voice. Stanley raised an uncertain hand to his lips to blow. The notes bubbled a clear and bright and haunting fountain. Soldier's ears pricked. Stanley blew again. Soldier cocked his head, then capered away to Rocket at the edge of the lake. It was a good whistle, Stanley was thinking, he'd cut it well. He stepped forward, smiling, holding out the whistle—then froze in Da's sudden, arctic glare.

"I'll drown it. Mark me, I'll drown it."

Stanley's heart thumped a tattoo. Da was stooping, fingering a stone. Stanley leaped toward Soldier. Da hurled the stone. It landed inches from Soldier in the shallows of the lake. Confounded with rage and disbelief, Stanley whirled around to his da. Throw a stone at a puppy? His own father? Then he could do it, would do it: would drown Soldier.

Da stomped away. Stanley turned back to Soldier and saw him, innocent and small and light against the deep, black water. In a vortex of horror and nausea, Stanley imagined a slender bubble rise on the surface of the lake, and another, and another—and a weighted sack dropping through dark water.

The twilight deepened. Still holding the rabbits, Stanley made his way to the game larder. When he'd skinned them, he turned to wash his bloodied hands. To the left of the sink, on the tiled wall above, hung a small mirror. Stanley was surprised by his reflection—did he really look so young? He leaned into the murky glass. A minute passed as he studied himself. His hair was too long and it flopped over his forehead. He straightened up. He was fourteen, but he was tall, taller almost than Tom. If he lifted his chin, squared his shoulders, could he look fifteen? Sixteen? Seventeen? What was the difference between a fourteen- and a seventeen-year-old face? Stanley rubbed his chin. A beard would help. If he looked older, he could enlist.

Also reflected in the glass were Tom's cap and coat, hanging on a nail. On an impulse, Stanley turned, crossed the room, unhooked them. He put on the cap and turned to the glass, pushing his hair off his face. Looking at himself from all sides, he tried the coat. The length of the sleeves was good, but it was broad across the chest. Stanley buttoned it and rubbed the dust from the glass with his cuff. That was better.

It wasn't easy, he thought, to tell what sort of age he was now. Anyway, all sorts of men had signed up. Shepherd, the old History teacher, had been too short in 1914, but then he'd been tall enough by 1916. Lara Bird's father was almost an old man but they'd taken him too. Recruitment officers were given a sixpence for every man they signed up—that's why they'd signed them up, because of the sixpence probably. Stanley stood to attention, clicked his heels and saluted, fingers to the edge of Tom's cap.

"Seventeen, sir."

Soldier leaped to his side and Stanley looked at him, distraught, realizing—you couldn't join the Army with a puppy. He couldn't join Tom.

No, he couldn't do that . . . but he and Soldier must leave at first light and take their chances together.

Early the next morning

Lancashire

A howl split the dawn. Stanley sprang out of bed and yanked the curtains open.

The coach-house doors were open, the trap gone. What was Da doing up so early? Tethered to the bars of the kennel was Rocket, her long neck outstretched. Her howls circled upward, haunting the thin air. The glistening cobbles reflected the shivering sky.

"I'll drown it. Mark me, I'll drown it."

Da's words were icy and precise in Stanley's head. A lightning surge of anger shot from his scalp to his fingertips. Fool, fool, fool! He should never have left Soldier alone, not for one minute; he should have slept in the stable, keeping guard.

Stanley hurled himself, missing, stumbling down the stairs, and charged into the yard. He flung the kennel gate open, slamming it against the stone wall. Scattered, broken straws were brown and sodden, trampled into the wooden boards, the hessian bedding gone—Da had taken the sack.

Rocket hurled out a primeval yowl, which juddered against the streaming buildings, and twisted the pit of Stanley's belly.

"I'll drown it. Mark me, I'll drown it."

He choked and gagged. The tiny dog with the oatmeal coat and whirring tail. Stanley ran barefoot, maddened, blistering. He saw a golden straw on the ground—straw from Soldier's bedding—and clutched it up. Following straws, he raced along Park Drive, stopping to grasp at them. On he ran, snatching at clues, a child on a sinister, demented treasure hunt. There—there were wheel marks tracking the mud. Stanley followed them, knowing where they'd lead.

At the far end of the lake stood the trap. There was Trumpet and there was Da—he'd seen Stanley, was leaping into the trap, lashing the old cob into a canter from a standing start. The trap disappeared into the dark spruce. Stanley ran screaming to the trap, running, still screaming, his feet bleeding. He heard the lash of a whip, Da's shout as he urged Trumpet on. Stanley stopped on the flattened grass where the trap had pulled up at the water's edge. Nauseous with horror, he moved slowly toward the edge of the lake, inching his eyes up from the trampled reeds to the stone ledge where the water was deepest. This was where he'd seen Da so often. Hour after hour, Da came and stood here; here, where the water was blackest, he'd chosen to drown the tiny Soldier. The surface was blank. Not a ripple. Stanley retched and turned and ran, howling, to the cottage.

Back in the yard, Stanley knelt by Rocket. He saw the rope that tethered her. Da might tether his dog but he couldn't tether his son. Stanley would leave, could never live with Da again, never pass that lake again. He put his cheek to Rocket's flawless coat and fingered her silky ears.

"Stay with Da. He does love you . . ."

Stanley yanked Tom's best coat and cap from the hook by the door and stuffed the postcard of the collie into his pocket. He slipped one of the reed whistles into a Bryant & May matchbox and that too he put in his pocket, flinging the second on to Da's red chair.

He emptied the tin of kitchen money, ripped a sheet of paper from his Grammar exercise book, and wrote:

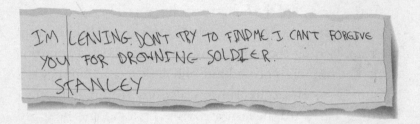

I'M LEAVING. DON'T TRY TO FIND ME. I CAN'T FORGIVE YOU FOR DROWNING SOLDIER.
  STANLEY

At the door, one hand in his pocket, Stanley stopped to look one last time at the room. He saw the whistle on the chair. Da would see the whistle his son had made him, might see in it all the love and hope he'd destroyed. The whistle in the matchbox—that one he'd keep himself, forever, in memory of Soldier.

PART II

Early afternoon, the same day

Liverpool

The bus pulled up in Queen Square. This was the last stop. Stanley was forty miles from home, forty miles from Da. Full of purpose, he stepped down. He'd enlist. There was no Soldier. There was nothing to hold him back. He'd join the Army, and he'd do it today. Streetcars and taxicabs trundled past. A huge poster—at least seven yards long—covered the side of a passing streetcar, presenting the silhouette of a muscular arm and a clenched fist, under it the words, "LEND YOUR STRONG RIGHT ARM TO YOUR COUNTRY. ENLIST NOW."

Kitchener, the Secretary of State for War, had asked for "Men, and still more men until the enemy is crushed." The Army was desperately short, and if it could take half the old folk in Longridge it could take him.

The crowd grew tighter, more concentrated. People were standing about, just waiting. Stanley stopped, glimpsing a vivid image over the heads of the crowd: an artillery team dashing into action under heavy fire. Other posters were plastered to the windows of the imposing building. In one, above the words "ENLIST TODAY," a soldier wore the laurel wreath and sphinx and red rose of the East Lancashires.

Tom's regiment. A line had formed in front of the building: a motley bunch, all shapes, sizes, heights, ages, and all at odds with the tall, fit figures in the posters. It was getting late, but if the line kept moving, Stanley would be seen today.

A corpulent officer, dressed in khaki, sat at a desk in a high-ceilinged, oak-paneled room, sifting papers with one hand, nursing his belly with the other. He was getting more than rations, Stanley thought, more than the four ounces of butter a week he and Da got. The officer kept his eyes on the papers as Stanley approached. Stanley's hands were sticky, his mouth dry.

"And what can I do for you?" The officer's tone was derisive.

"I've c-c—" Stanley fought for air.

The officer's pen tap-tap-tapped the desk. Stanley took a deep breath.

"I've c-come to j-join up, sir."

"Name? Trade?" The voice was weary.

"S-Stanley Ryder, sir. Under-gardener, sir. And I help with the h-horses." Stanley looked at the floor. What was he thinking coming here? The officer raised a pair of red-veined eyes.

"Age?"

Stanley hesitated, floored by a sudden thought—was it a criminal offense to lie to the Army about your age?

"Sixteen, sir."

He bit his lip. You had to be *seventeen*. Why hadn't he said "Seventeen"? Seventeen was no more of a lie than sixteen.

The officer heaved an exasperated, over-loud sigh and scratched his forehead. Stanley's age seemed to have brought on a sudden headache.

Stanley didn't move. "Seventeen, sir, seventeen," he wanted to say. The officer closed his eyes and rolled his aching head from side to side.

"Will you go outside, turn around three times, and come back at five when you'll be seventeen?" The officer's belly rose and fell like a tug in a swell as he enjoyed his own joke.

"Yes, sir. Oh, yes, sir. Qu-quick-sticks, sir—right away, sir."

Stanley hurried out. He looked up and down the street for a clock. If the officer wanted him to return at five, he'd do exactly that. Half past four. Only half an hour till he was the right age.

At five, the officer raised his eyes and appraised Stanley as though inspecting a horse.

"Age?"

"Seventeen, sir."

"Hmm. Does your mother know you're seventeen?" he asked, mocking.

"She's dead, sir."

"I'm sorry. Well, 'under-gardener' you said, and—er—'horses.' There's no call for chrysanthemums in Flanders, but the Engineers are short of men that know about animals. Now, you could do us both a favor by saying you know about horses?"

"Oh, y-yes, sir. I do know about horses, sir."

"Good. Well done. Now, join the Royal Engineers."

Stanley was waved aside to an adjoining room and a

medical officer. Two men, both white as quartz, stood waiting, in their drawers. Stanley stripped and waited too.

A doctor entered the room, holding a tape measure in his hand, assessed them all with a despairing glance, and headed for Stanley. He looped the tape around Stanley's chest and brought his head close. The measure didn't seem to show the number he was looking for. He made a careful loop and clamped the loop between his thumb and index finger. This time the tape came to the right number and he noted the result with an exhausted exhalation.

Stanley was motioned on to the scales. The doctor's head almost touched the dial as Stanley again fell short of Army requirements. Another exhausted sigh. The doctor reached for a large blue dictionary and passed it to Stanley, then bent to read the result. Perfect. The combined weight of Stanley and the dictionary were recorded. Stanley's height was measured. The short-sighted eyes blinked in exaggerated surprise as Stanley appeared to have exceeded the minimum height regulation.

"A-one," the doctor muttered with a sardonic laugh and moved on to the next man.

In a daze, Stanley joined the blur of men around the desk, raised his hand, and swore his oath to King and country. He was a member of His Majesty's Army, and had a number. He was seventeen, had a railway warrant, and would be paid on Fridays.

By six o'clock the next morning, Stanley was two hundred miles from Da. He was on parade and his training had begun.

10 September 1917

Chatham, Kent

The vast and bleak parade ground was surrounded by barracks, offices, and the entrance gates. Fear kept drawing Stanley's eyes, like the needle of a compass, toward the gates. Da might stomp through them at any minute, shouting for all to hear, "Fourteen! The daft twerp's only fourteen!" Da would see the ill-fitting uniform, see the pants which billowed around his son's buttocks, see the puttee—the bandage-type stocking—that was in danger of unwinding at his right ankle, already unraveling at his knee. Da would mock him and haul him home. Stanley scanned the faces of the new recruits. No, no one here looked as young as he did.

"Parade, 'shun! Left turn! Quick march! Double! Left, right, left, right. Pick up your knees. Left, right, left, right . . ."

Company Sergeant-Major Quigley had a stout neck, an athletic figure, hair as glossy as a blackbird, and a ferocious moustache with long waxy ends that sometimes took on a life of their own. His tongue was like a rasp—his voice could probably be heard a mile away. The man was in his element, born to lead this 6 a.m. PT parade, but he was also a sort of relic, left over, perhaps, from an earlier war.

Stanley's eyes flickered toward the gates. Even if Da did come, Stanley would never go home again.

"Double! Left, right, left, right . . ."

A smile played on Quigley's lips as he increased the pace. Stanley's puttee was unraveling further.

"Double! Left-right-left-right-left-right-left-right . . ." Quigley's foghorn voice belted out instructions faster and faster until the men were racing around the yard. Stanley couldn't concentrate because of the unraveling puttee. Quigley would spot him and single him out, would know he was too young and send him home. At least Stanley had a uniform, and a cap—half of the men were still in mufti, as home clothes were known here. It wasn't like the pictures and the posters, this lack of beds and plates and uniforms.

Everyone had about-turned except Stanley, who found himself face to face with Hamish McManus. Hamish had the bed next to Stanley. That morning, no one else had spoken to Stanley, but Hamish, with a frank and friendly smile, had said, "Watch out for yourself, laddie. They'd steal the milk from a baby's bottle here."

Now Hamish put a hand on Stanley's shoulder to turn him around, but not before Quigley had seen Stanley facing the wrong way. Quigley marched over, eyes sparking, and halted uncomfortably close to Stanley.

"Get that hair cut. Are you a soldier, hmm, or an artist? Get some fluff on that upper lip before I see you again." Stanley felt the man's breath on his face as his baton prodded the troublesome puttee.

"Your mother won't be here, hmm, from now on, to dress you in the mornings."

"N-no, sir." There it was again, that dryness, the splintering words. "This p-pair of pants is too loose, sir."

"Speak English, damn you." Quigley looked so bewildered that perhaps he hadn't heard Stanley properly, but now he recovered his flow. "Choirboys and milksops, that's what I've been sent." Quigley's moustache twitched with mirth. "And if any of you want to go home, hmm, and see your m-mothers again, I'll first make soldiers of you"—his voice rose—"or I'll die in the attempt."

Someone on the other side of the yard tittered. Quigley swiveled on a sixpence, nimble enough to catch a smirk on the face of a tall, thin man.

"And I'll teach you not to laugh on parade, Fidget! I don't want to see a smile on your milk-white mug till kingdom come."

Stanley felt a gentle squeeze on his shoulder, and turned. Hamish smiled at him, a warm, tranquil smile, and whispered, "The Sergeant-Major's just a bully, laddie, just a bully."

Yes, thought Stanley, just a bully. I've left home, left one bully only to run into another.

"Everyone. On all fours. Now, up-down, up-down, up-down . . ."

Stanley's eyes watered as pain seared his muscles. He must blot out the burning pain in his arms. He closed his eyes, and at once visions of Soldier and of the dark lake flooded his head. A solitary circle rose on the surface of the water that he saw in his mind. It rippled outward, unleashing a tidal wave of anger that surged through Stanley. Charged with raging pain, on he went, up-down, up-down, till he was the last man still going.

Six weeks inched past. Stanley had got used to Quigley's mockery, got used to the food, to the rules and the regulations of Army life. If he wasn't hopping up and down, he was being inspected. He was always being inspected. Everything had to be done just so, blankets folded just so, shoes shined just so.

"Subservience and obedience, laddie," Hamish had said to him as they'd folded their blankets. "They want them to run in your blood." Hamish was right, in the Army you must never think for yourself and you must always obey, however pointless the exercise. You must always have shiny boots or be punished with three days on water and biscuits if they told you to. Stanley would keep on doing everything just so, keep his head low, his boots clean, his blankets folded and he'd eventually be sent to France, where Tom was—and Quigley wasn't.

Hamish and his brother, James, were both in Stanley's unit. They were both clear-browed, large men, born to big hills and deep valleys. James, the older of the two, was a little morose, but Stanley liked and trusted them both.

Everyone was progressing to specialist training. For Stanley there'd be two extra weeks of parade drills, bayonet fighting, musketry, route marching, wheeling about to the right and the left, inclining and forming squads. He alone among his batch of recruits had been ordered to do two more weeks of Basic Training. Two weeks longer to get to France.

Stanley's companions were lining up for the canteen, their mood jubilant. There'd been a success in France at Cambrai.

Church bells had rung today for the first time. Had Tom been there, at Cambrai? The country had clutched at something to celebrate after Passchendaele. One hundred and forty thousand casualties for a five-mile advance. Had Tom been there at Passchendaele?

As each man turned the corner into the canteen, he looked at a list pinned to the Orderly Room door. That was how you knew if you had a parcel, but Stanley never looked. There'd never be a parcel for him, so it was better not to think about it, better just to concentrate on counting days.

"Stanley, have they sent you anything?" James and Hamish were both looking at the notice. Stanley shook his head and turned away. Hamish and James might get parcels of jam and chocolate, Stanley was thinking, but he never would. Not till Tom knew where he was.

"No one knows, do they, that you're here?" said Hamish quietly. Not expecting an answer, he continued, "But we know, and we'll take care of you."

Stanley took a place at a table next to Hamish, opposite James. James picked up the loaf of bread.

"Made of grit and granite," he said, weighing it in his hand before passing it to Stanley. "Needs lots of margarine so it's easier to chew."

The surface of the table was swimming in sloshed tea. Each man slopped tea into his jar from a basin in the middle of the table. Tea wasn't at its best in a jam jar, but when you were tired it was good that it was strong and sweet. The tall man, called Fidget, who'd snickered on parade that first morning, slipped himself in between Stanley and Hamish and placed a parcel on the table where everyone could see it. All of Fidget was long and colorless, like a weed grown too fast in a dark cupboard, and he had a habit of sliding into places where he wasn't especially welcome. Fidget's hands fluttered over his parcel. His darting gooseberry eyes widened, and his mouth opened to a slack smile.

"From my sister . . . She sends one every week. Fruit cake." The loose smile was interrupted by a sudden thought. "Do you get parcels, Stanley?"

Fidget's face was too mobile, his eyes the color of Army tea. Fidget meant no harm but, unable to answer, Stanley looked down. He scribbled with his forefinger in the tea on the table.

"Do you get parcels, Stanley?" asked Fidget once more.

The doodle in the tea had a tail and a long snout.

"Don't say much, do you, Stanley Ryder?"

Once upon a time, Stanley was thinking, there'd been tablecloths and honey and a mother to make cakes. Once there'd been a beautiful oatmeal puppy . . .

Fidget wasn't to be put off. "She's a good cook, my sister. Is your mother a good cook?"

If Stanley answered, his words would stick in his throat. His forefinger wiped out the dog in the tea. Ma had been a lovely cook. Stanley swallowed hard.

Hamish put an arm around Stanley's shoulder. "Come on, Stanley. The cake in the YMCA hut's better than Army food any day. We're parading for pay tomorrow, and I've got money over from last week."

Stanley shot Hamish a grateful smile, and they rose and left. As they made their way past the rank and file of tables, Hamish asked, "Do you like dogs?"

Stanley felt the death of Soldier jam like a stone in his throat. He said nothing. Hamish tightened his arm around the boy's shoulders and steered him on. It was good, Stanley felt, to be with Hamish, who was kind and thoughtful, and never minded that Stanley said so little. At the Orderly Room door, Hamish said, "Did you see this?"

Stanley's throat constricted as he saw the mail list.

"Not that." Hamish pointed. "*This*. Read this. Working with dogs would be more fun than tunneling with the Engineers—aye, and safer. What do you think?"

Stanley felt Hamish's gentle eyes on him as he read:

THE MESSENGER DOG SERVICE REQUIRES MEN ACCUSTOMED TO WORKING WITH ANIMALS TO VOLUNTEER.

THOSE INTERESTED TO APPLY TO SGT. QUIGLEY

Dogs? Messenger dogs? How wonderful, Stanley was thinking, wonderful beyond imagining. Yes, he thought, I'd love that.

"You'll have had reasons of your own for signing up, and I'll ask no questions, but the Front will be no place for you, laddie. The Dog Service maybe would be just the ticket for you."

Stanley spread his uniform out on the bed, admiring the "R.E." on the collar and the embroidered flags, the proud insignia of the Royal Engineers, on the left arm. This week had been a good week. Twenty-eight men had been requested for Signal School and Quigley had instructed Stanley to sign up and do it before his transfer to the Messenger Dog School. Stanley liked Signaling—he liked the lamps and the heliographs and wires. He'd learned that signaling was vital in a war that was trench-based, where so much depended now on messages being sent to and from the front lines. Those messages sent by telegram, dispatch rider, radio, by telephone, wireless, or pigeon, could make the difference to the success or failure of an operation, and Stanley was proud to be part of the Signals Service. He'd done well, too— he'd passed first-class in the Signaling Examination and now he had a new issue: a greatcoat. He was proud of the coat, proud of his regiment, of its history, its dignity, and importance. Stanley smoothed the sleeve with the embroidered flags.

A desolate Christmas had come and gone, and still Stanley had heard nothing from Da, from Tom. Had no one even tried to find him? he wondered, as his fingers traced the "R.E." They'd be amazed, Da and Tom both, if they knew. He'd like them to see him on parade. Stanley's eyes flickered to the window, and the gates beyond, recognizing now, as he looked, that it was hope that drew his eyes to the gates, hope that Da might come. He'd been here one hundred days exactly and there'd been no word from Da.

If Stanley went to the War Dog School, he'd most likely be detailed to the Western Front and, if he kept his fingers crossed, to France. He wouldn't write to Tom, not until he got to France. If he wrote before then, Tom might write to Da and get him sent back home. Tom wouldn't think that his little brother's having enlisted was a good thing: "I will always be thankful," his postcard had said, "that you were too young to fight." Face to face with Tom, Stanley could explain how things had been at home, why he'd had to leave.

Stanley turned from the window, wondering how old Soldier would have been by now, what sort of dog he'd have turned out to be. With a strained glance at the mirror by the door, he straightened his cap.

The six men waiting outside Quigley's office were clustered around a cutting pinned to the door:

DOGS FOR THE ARMY.

The War Office requires a further gift of dogs for military purposes. Particulars of the animals required are as follows:—Breeds: Danes, Mastiffs, St. Bernards, Newfoundlands, Bull Mastiffs, Retrievers, Collies, Sheepdogs, large curs, Dalmatians, Lurchers, Airedales, crossbred shepherds. No dogs smaller than Airedale Terriers are required. Age, between eighteen months and five years. Sex: No bitches required, only dogs. Dogs should be in the first place offered to the Commandant, War Dog School, Shoeburyness. If accepted and approved of, instructions will be sent for forwarding, and any dogs found unsuitable after testing will be returned to their owners, carriage paid.

Why had dogs been killed when the Army needed them? "Bang. Gone. Horse-meat for France." Da had been right to be so angry.

When they were seated, Quigley addressed them. Here, off the parade ground, the man seemed a little diminished.

"Your time here has only a few days left to run, gentlemen. You are shortly to receive your transfer to Shoeburyness in Essex." The Sergeant-Major's eyes took on a mocking glint. "Five weeks seems to be required for the, hmm, Messenger Dog Service."

Five more weeks, Stanley was thinking, so long till I go to France.

"This service is a new division of the Signals Service, which as you know, is itself a division of the Royal Engineers. Unike all other Signals Service recruits, you'll no longer be known as Pioneers—but as *Keepers*." Quigley's brows rose in open mockery. "Colonel Edwin Hautenville Richardson has been badgering the War Office since 1914 to use his dogs. Well, two of his dogs were trialled by the Royal Artillery, and it appears that they carried messages successfully, so the War Office has allowed him to establish a Dog School."

Messages? Stanley was puzzled and captivated. How wonderful—to use dogs as messengers!

"If you fail your training there, you will be returned here."

I will not, Stanley thought, watching the gleaming moustache twitch, ever come back here; I will never fall into your hands to be bullied again.

7 January 1918

Essex

Ten new recruits sat on a series of wooden benches ranged around a dais in front of a window, waiting for the Colonel. Their rough hands, frugal speech, and broad faces suggested they were countrymen, ghillies maybe, or farmers or huntsmen.

Through the window, in the last of the day's light, Stanley saw two fields striped with orderly rows of wooden kennels. The Messenger Dog School was bounded to the east by the sea, to the north by the river. An immense sky dominated the low-lying land, all reclaimed salt marsh, interrupted by hedgerows of scrub elm, ditches and dykes, and then the tidal mudflats.

A red admiral, early to arrive, was resting on the window ledge. On its folded wings Stanley saw the flashes of orange red. Stanley would let it out—could do it quickly before the Colonel came in. He rose and moved toward the window. He captured the butterfly, feeling, in the bowl of his palm, its furry thorax and the panicked batting of its powerful wings.

Brisk steps sounded along the corridor. Stanley lifted the sash window and stretched out his arm. The door opened and closed. There were footsteps behind him and Stanley was joined at the window. He opened his palm and glimpsed the black and white tracery of the admiral's wings as it looped and curved away.

"Do you know, that tiny wingspan's no more than seven centimeters . . ." The voice was entranced and gentle. "He weighs perhaps less than two rose petals, but if he hasn't overwintered here, he'll have been all the way to Spain or France." Stanley turned to face a silver-haired man with a noble nose and stern, periwinkle eyes. He saw too, the Colonel's smile waver, his eyes sharpen and his arms fall in a gesture of anger and despair. The Colonel turned abruptly. Stanley remembered Quigley's taunts about his age, remembered the McManus brothers and their fatherly watchfulness, and realized, hurrying to his bench, that they all knew at a glance that he was underage.

Colonel Richardson took the dais and began to speak, his manner courteous but firm. "Gentlemen, you are here on probation. I accept only men of the highest character. It is your solemn obligation to display only the qualities you'd like to see in your dogs, because a dog that lives with a man of pluck and courage will itself become plucky and courageous . . ."

The Colonel's eagle eyes scanned the room, boring into the heart of each recruit, weighing him and assessing him, but always overlooking Stanley. Stanley sat up straight, defiant and intent.

"I'll be training you and you'll be training the dogs. You must forget anything that you've ever learned. I don't want experience . . . I simply want a natural love of dogs."

Stanley watched the Colonel, challenging him to meet his eyes. He, Stanley, more than anyone here, had a natural love of dogs. He would not be treated as a child . . .

"Your dogs are new here too. Since arriving, they've had twenty-four hours' isolation and forty-eight hours' rest. They've been dipped and disinfected by Macy, our veterinary head nurse. They've been given a leather collar, a tin message-cylinder, a brass tag engraved with 'WAR MESSENGER DOG' and a number."

As the Colonel paused, Stanley heard the thudding of heavy guns from the nearby Artillery practice ground.

"You'll each be allocated three dogs. Each dog will have one master. One man and only one man will be his master. You will make each and every thing about his working day a pleasure and a joy to him. You'll teach him to be a soldier, to have discipline and sang-froid. If a dog is lazy, greedy, or cowardly, if he lacks focus or concentration, he will be returned home. Those of you that do well will, when the time comes, serve a fortnight at a time, twelve hours a day, in the front-line trenches with your dogs." Still the Colonel was avoiding Stanley, though the boy kept his eyes firmly fixed on him, willing the Colonel to meet his gaze.

Colonel Richardson faced the line of keepers, at his heels a bewildered rabble of dogs, some scrawny, some stout, some tall, whimpering like new children on their first day at school. In the field beyond, chained to their kennels, the experienced dogs, the old hands, snouts held high, surveyed the new recruits—both the men and the new dogs—with silent skepticism.

Stanley would be the last to get his dogs. Starting at the far end of the line, Lance-Corporal Birdwood, known to the men as Birdie, had begun to distribute them.

Birdie and the Colonel were nearing the end of the line. There were two men left to go—Trigger Doyle and Stanley—but only four dogs left in the Colonel's hands. Were there not enough dogs to go around? Perhaps they'd each have only two dogs. A racy-looking Airedale was still there, along with two very tall dogs and a teddy-bearish sheepdog. Which would be his, and which would be Doyle's? Stanley glanced sideways at the short, wiry Doyle. His complexion was rough but despite that, and his confidence, he was perhaps as young as Stanley himself. Watching him, Stanley wondered if perhaps Doyle had stood on a pile of books in the recruiting office. Last night he'd introduced himself as "Trigger—Trigger Doyle," and he'd winked at Stanley with a complicity that Stanley didn't quite like.

"Dog number 2154," said Richardson. The Colonel cast a paternal eye over the sheepdog Birdie was giving to Trigger. "Pharaoh . . . He's got brains—that big square skull has plenty of room for brainpower."

Stanley looked at the rough-and-tumble dog, at the intelligent beam of his eyes beneath the grizzled fringe, and felt a prick of envy. He looked at the remaining dogs. What would be left for him? Not the Airedale—Birdie was already handing him to Trigger—but the huge brindled dog was still there, and so was the tall wheaten one.

"This is Bandit. An Airedale," the Colonel was saying. "He'll be a soldier through and through, spirited, loyal, and ridiculously brave." Stanley glanced at the gallant, dashing

Bandit then his eyes shot back to the Colonel, his heart in his mouth.

Birdie was giving Trigger another dog—the handsome, bearded, wheaten one. Stanley bit his lip. There was only to be one for him—the brindled one, striped like a tiger in brown and gold. There were not enough dogs to go around and the Colonel had picked Stanley to receive only one. That truculent giant had been picked especially for him. His chance of getting to France would be hopeless with just one dog. With that dog.

Richardson moved along to Stanley. Stanley straightened up and squared his shoulders, defying the Colonel to look at him. The Colonel read from his ledger. "Bones."

"Dog number 2153," said Birdie.

"Bones . . . A great Dane . . . a headlong mountain of a dog, this one. Well, do your best . . . It'll be hard to win his trust—he was a guard dog. Then he was abandoned—like so many others—because of rationing, because his owners couldn't feed him. He's a suspicious animal, mistrustful. He'll be a difficult case but try to channel that ferocity of his."

The Colonel's eyes finally rose from Bones to Stanley, then shifted to the middle distance. Birdie handed Stanley a lead as the Colonel continued, "You see, I'm forced to take whatever comes. I just can't get enough good dogs." He took a long sad breath. "I'm still applying for more and, well, they might still come in." He looked again at Bones and said, "Bones might well be unsuitable for this kind of work. Danes make better tracking dogs than messenger dogs, but, well, let's see—you know, if a dog loves you, he'll do anything for you."

The Colonel was on the point of saying more when he looked again directly at Stanley and paused. With a sorrowful shake of his head, he thought better of whatever he was going to say, turned to Birdie and, as they walked away, Stanley caught the drift of his whispered words.

"It's not right . . . so young . . ." Still shaking his head, the Colonel made his way back to the center of the line. "Fidelity. Courage. Honor. These are the qualities we hope to find in a dog, these and the homing instinct. Now, this instinct exists in all dogs, but the cultivation of it will form the kernel of your training here."

Stanley looked at Bones. The showy black and brown brindle of Bones's coat had the dangerous sheen of a savage and unpredictable jungle animal. Headstrong, thought Stanley, seeing the deep jaws, the incisors that could rip anything to shreds. Stanley wondered whether he did, after all, have a natural love of dogs, because if he had, it seemed to have deserted him now. It was the bulk and heft of Bones that was so off-putting. Da's dogs had always been as light as shadows and he could feel nothing but revulsion for this drooling giant.

As the Colonel spoke, a self-important young plover with browny-grey winter plumage trotted urgently across the sand a few feet away. Bones cocked his large head, brows raised appealingly, ears pricked, all that surly truculence suddenly evaporated. He raised a stout forepaw as if to play. The dog had no more sense than a skittle, thought Stanley, exasperated, watching Bones paw the ground in invitation to the plover. The bird trotted off. Bones's head drooped, his eyes blinking mournfully in the direction of the now distant plover. It amused Stanley that Bones looked marvellously ferocious but was really so gentle.

"Silly Bones."

The triangular ears collapsed, downcast against his cheeks. That head was so expressive, the fleeting changes from surly suspicion to playfulness to disappointment, all so easily read, and Stanley was surprised to feel a glimmer of affection for this clumsy, playful giant.

Richardson was still speaking.

"Dogs are four times faster than humans. They can swim across shell holes and canals. They can find their way at night and run as fast at night as by day. They are not shell-shy. They can exercise the homing instinct within only one week of arriving at a new area, picking up one individual scent and following it—despite thousands of competing smells—across ground that is impassable for horse, man, or machine."

Stanley smiled to see yet another sudden change in Bones, now sitting as tall and still as an imperial statue. Stanley noticed the surprising majesty of him, the acute sense he had of his own dignity.

"Bones," whispered Stanley.

The dog's high, close-set ears tightened so that they touched each other, twin sails atop his square skull. He smacked his jowls and blinked up at Stanley, then shuffled his haunches back to sit on Stanley's toes, nestling against Stanley's legs.

"The dog must want to be with you. If he wants to be with you," Richardson was saying, "then he will be faithful, courageous, and honorable. Not only that, but he'll be pulled, as though by magnetism, through falling bombs, through hurricanes of fire, and fields of rolling tanks, by his longing to be with you. If he loves you, he will rush home to you, even through blizzards of flying steel."

"Flying steel." Stanley took a deep breath, and whispered to Bones, "We will do it together, and show them all, you and I."

The dog cast his head around, saw Pharaoh, set his jaws, and began a deep, grumbling growl. A little intimidated, Pharaoh's large, soft paws edged backward. Stanley smiled— Bones was guarding him, all of his great weight now leaning as heavily and defensively as a bulwark against Stanley's legs. Stanley braced himself against the weight of the dog, a little charmed by the dog's ready acceptance of his new master, and his determination to protect him.

"Yes," he breathed, "you will be faithful, courageous, and honorable." He looked up at the Colonel, and added, with a flint of anger, "Or we will never get to France and to Tom."

The days raced by.

Each day the six-thirty reveille was followed by roll call at seven, then breakfast. At eight the keepers groomed the dogs. At nine there was a general parade of staff, trainers, orderlies, keepers, and highly excited dogs. The rest of the day was spent on fitness exercises and the Homing Instinct run with only one hour free before the evening lecture.

After three weeks of fitness training, the first of the war training exercises, the Firing Infantry, had been introduced. This would accustom the dogs to rifle fire. Two days ago there'd been just one gun, yesterday two. Today there'd be six infantrymen. Stanley joined the line of keepers standing a couple hundred feet away from a row of infantry. The Colonel's orderlies approached to lead the dogs away to their far side. At Birdie's whistle the dogs would be released, the infantry would fire blanks, and the dogs were to run into the firing line and through to their keepers.

Bones's rumbling purr cranked up. The closer the orderly came, the louder his growl. Stanley cuffed him around the ears. Bones looked up briefly, clamping his jaws in injured pride before turning again, unable to suppress a final warning growl.

"You big silly," Stanley said grinning. "Don't be so suspicious." Bones's round eyes shot up to his master, confused, then back to the oncoming danger.

"No, Bones. No. We're going to walk through the village again this afternoon, and we'll keep on and on, until you learn not to guard me but to come home to me." Bones shuffled back against Stanley, rump on Stanley's feet, head against his hip bone, intermittent rumblings still escaping. Stanley handed the lead over to the orderly.

"Leave," Stanley commanded. Bones looked up, mystified. Was Stanley really sure, those chestnut eyes asked: was it not madness to go off with someone else?

"Leave."

Bones leaped up good-naturedly and loped away with his springy, easy gait to take his place beyond the infantry.

Stanley scuffed the grass with his boot. Yesterday Bones had advanced, then reversed, casting around for a way to Stanley which avoided the infantry. When he'd found none, the pack instinct had tugged him forward with the other dogs into the storm of blanks. Bones was willful, but he must do what was asked of him, not what he thought best.

A whistle blew. The infantry burst into fire. It was hard, in the smoke and confusion, to see what was happening, but there—there was the first dog, already on the near side. Stanley searched the flurry of dogs tearing home. No Bones. Now that the smoke was beginning to lift, Stanley could see the line of orderlies beyond the riflemen. Bones wasn't among them, nor among the rush of tail-wagging dogs greeting their keepers. Stanley felt a flicker of irritation that all Doyle's dogs had arrived home. Where had Bones gone? Stanley whirled around and Bones hurled himself at him, breathless and slobbering and frantic with pride, looking as though he might vault into the boy's arms. Bones had gone the long way around behind the shed, avoiding the gunfire, coming up at Stanley from behind, but Stanley saw the pride in his shining, black-rimmed eyes, and his exasperation melted at the sheer charm of the dog, at his child-like exuberance.

"Sit," commanded Stanley with his hand only. Bones chomped and slathered, and reluctantly sat, waiting for his reward. Stanley kept his hand raised; there'd be no reward this time. Bones snuffled Stanley's pocket for his titbit.

"No," said Stanley. "You'll go back and do it again, until you get it right."

Bones was taken forward again and again, but each time avoided the guns. Stanley's tone grew firmer. Once again Stanley signaled for an orderly to collect Bones. All the other men and dogs had finished, leaving only Stanley, the orderly, Bones, and the infantry in the gathering dusk.

"Wait," Stanley called, racing up behind the orderly. "I'll go with him. I'll walk through the guns with him, I'll show him myself what he must do."

"Are you sure, Keeper Ryder?"

Stanley braced himself as he looked toward the sinister barrels of the rifles, and nodded. He didn't want to but he would—to show Bones. They took their place beyond the infantry. The orderly blew a whistle, released Bones's lead.

"Come, Bones, come. Follow me." Stanley started off at a run. The blanks and the noise wouldn't hurt him any more than they'd hurt Bones. Stanley tensed as the guns burst into fire, but forced himself onward into the red flashes of red and the noise, Bones loping cheerfully along at his side.

They'd reached the line and gone through. As they reached their post, Stanley raised his hand, then held out some chopped liver, saying, "Good boy, good. Now, go, Bones, on your own now. The way I showed you."

"Last time," shouted the infantry officer, checking his watch, as the orderly collected Bones. The dog took his place. Stanley kept his eyes on him, willing Bones to do what was asked.

"Come, Bones, come," he breathed. The whistle blew and Bones was released. Bones paused, forepaw raised and hesitant, his expressive head cast in an unusually thoughtful attitude. Bones, thought Stanley, smiling, was not a dog much given to thoughtfulness. Bones was loping forward now, not step by trembling step as the other dogs had run into the guns, but with playful, headlong nonchalance.

That evening the Colonel sought Stanley out in the canteen and told him that he must continue for another week on the Firing Drill, while other men progressed to the Heavy Guns. Bones had to be very clear, the Colonel said, what was expected of him. After all they'd gone through that day, Stanley gritted his teeth.

"Yes, sir," Stanley said as gamely as he could manage. He wouldn't be beaten, he would do whatever it took.

Stanley's personal frustration was echoed in the prevailing mood of the country. The New Year had brought new depths of gloom and despair. The Hun had come back after Cambrai with a tiger's pounce and now those church bells looked premature and foolish.

Day after day went by in this way until the Colonel signaled, with a forced and silent nod, to move them on to the Heavy Guns. Bones was used to the distant thundering of the guns, but today he'd be no more than twelve feet away from them and must remain calm and still as they pounded away.

Stanley stood waiting with Bones, his pockets full of chopped liver, ready to distract the dog if he took fright at the heavies. Bones was alert, his close-set ears pricked high. Stanley eyed the eighteen-pounders nervously. At a signal the gunners burst into fire, and Stanley held his hands up against the deafening roar. Bones launched his entire bulk at Stanley as though to leap into his arms. Boy and dog fell together, tangled on the damp grass, Bones trying to bury himself beneath Stanley, the ground rattling under them, but now Bones was snuffling at the liver in Stanley's pocket. Stanley laughed despairingly, disentangled himself, and sat up. Bones let a distracted growl escape in the direction of the guns, then nosed again at Stanley's pockets.

"Big silly," Stanley said. "Sit." Bones sat, growling sporadically at the guns, chains of saliva swinging greedily from his jowls. Stanley fed him a titbit. "Good boy," he kept whispering.

On and on went the hurricane of ear-scorching fire. Only Bones among the fretful, unsettled animals sat firm, head up, highly conscious of his own majesty and dreaming of raw liver.

After another week, Stanley and Bones moved on to Bomb Drill. As they joined the circle of men and dogs around a deep pit, Richardson addressed the keepers.

"This is the third exercise in preparation for No Man's Land, and is designed to accustom the dogs to mortar bombs. At my first whistle, the orderlies will throw raw meat into the pit. At my second, they'll throw dummy mortar bombs on to the surrounding area. At my third, you will release your dogs. This training will be very gradual. Don't speak roughly to your dogs. If a dog fails, take him back to try again, and if he does it well, if he eats from the pit, reward him."

Stanley eyed the vicious-looking grenades the orderlies held. He looked at Bones sitting statue still. Next to Bones were Trigger Doyle and his dogs, keeping, like everyone else, a respectful berth around Bones. Stanley liked Trigger, liked that Trigger took everyone as they came, not minding that Stanley didn't talk much. Trigger said he worked as a ghillie, but Stanley wasn't sure, thought there was something raggedy, perhaps, about Trigger's morals. More poacher than ghillie, Stanley thought to himself. Still, he liked Trigger.

A whistle went and the horseflesh was thrown into the

pit. At once, the circle of dogs, though still to heel, grew restless. Bones's snout quivered but he remained sitting, awaiting Stanley's command. A few minutes passed and now he began to lose his self-control, half rising and turning, half sitting. He looked at Stanley, reproachfully cocking his head and turning another circle, still crouching, saliva glittering in the sun and swirling out like the chains of a merry-go-round. It was taking all of Stanley's strength now to hold him back. Trigger watched Stanley, laughing, but Stanley thought that Trigger was perhaps a tiny bit jealous, too, of the majestic Bones.

"Sit, Bones."

Richardson was speaking. "The older dogs will do the training and you'll again see the pack instinct at work. Your dogs would rather brave the unknown—in this case, the grenades—than let other dogs get all the meat." He smiled, put his whistle to his mouth and blew.

The orderlies, standing between the keepers and the pit, lit their fuses and threw the grenades.

"Get on," Stanley whispered to Bones, slipping his collar. The fuses took no more than five seconds to burn, then came the ear-splitting noise—no smoke, no flashes, just noise. Bones was halfway to the pit when he whipped around. Stanley raised a hand to stop him.

The dog's ears were pricked, his tail lifted like a saber, his coat bristling at the neck. Already the experienced dogs were through the grenades, hurling themselves into the pit, flinging themselves on to the meat; some of the new dogs, too. Trigger's deer-hound, Gypsy, was in already, others following more cautiously.

Bones growled again in the direction of the explosions, placing himself firmly between his master and the bombs.

"They won't hurt me. Don't worry about me. Get on, Bones, get on . . ."

Bones hesitated, then started forward on his catlike paws, his springy step turning to a bounding run, like the bouncing gait of a thoroughbred horse. The dog was fearless; it was just his instinct to guard that formed his biggest challenge.

Later that afternoon Stanley scrubbed the kennel as Bones waited outside, muscular as a prizefighter, proud as a peacock, surveying his field. Everyone else had three kennels to clean while Stanley only had the one. Trigger would say cheerfully that there'd be more dogs along soon for Stanley, but Trigger didn't really know.

Stanley looked at Bones and wondered about the breeding that had produced such a specimen. Perhaps Da had been right after all to value pure-bloods above all else? Of a sudden, Stanley felt guilty that since having Bones he'd thought so little of Soldier. Now visions came racing back—Soldier cavorting in Trumpet's stable—the sable eyes and porridge coat—and, flooded with raging anger, Stanley vowed he'd never, ever forgive what Da had done.

Macy, the head nurse, was on his evening round, inspecting the condition of each dog. Bones rose, growling, high-set ears pricked.

"Shh. It's only Macy, come to check you over."

Before Macy began his inspection, Stanley would ask him the question that mattered so much.

"W-will the C-colonel give me another dog, Macy? He won't send me to France with only one dog, will he?"

Macy hesitated, sighed, and interrupted his examination of Bones's forepaw. "If Russia and Germany sign a peace treaty, Keeper Ryder, we'll be vastly outnumbered—those troops from the Eastern front all free . . . it'll be no place—"

"I have to go, Macy. I have to go—" The desperate note in his own voice stopped Stanley short and made Macy look up sharply.

"The Colonel will have reasons of his own for not wanting you to go to France, Ryder . . ."

Bones was half growling, half purring, losing the battle for self-control, his tail poised to wag but his hackles prickling too. There behind Macy was the Colonel.

Stanley rose and faced the Colonel. They were the same height and Stanley met him eye to eye. "I want two more dogs, sir."

The Colonel paused, taken aback by Stanley's anger. When he answered it was with anger of his own. "We're short, Ryder. Now the officers have seen the dogs in action and know they can save the lives of human runners"—the Colonel's blue eyes sparked—"now they're crying out for them. But it's too late, I can't get any more. I've been waiting three weeks . . . nothing. I've put calls on the wireless, in the newspapers. We had twelve thousand dogs handed in, but there are so few left . . . so many were shot, put down, abandoned."

Stanley was thinking of Da's rant, about hounds being shot.

"I've placed a new advertisement." The Colonel handed

Stanley a cutting from his pocket. "We're doing everything
we can . . ."

A photograph of Richardson led the news item, followed
by the words, "THE WAR OFFICE REQUIRES A FUR-
THER GIFT OF DOGS FOR MILITARY PURPOSES."

**Our women have given their husbands, their
sons, their fathers, their brothers—and now,
their dogs. Twelve thousand dogs have been
handed in so far, an overwhelming response.
But still more are needed. There have been
several calls on the wireless for the public to
donate their dogs. We have already taken dogs
from the Dogs Homes at Leeds and Battersea—**

Stanley looked up impatiently, handing the cutting back.
"Will you send me to F-France with only one dog?"

The Colonel was silent a moment. When he answered, it
was with more sorrow than anger. "No, Ryder. With only
one dog, I won't, if I can help it, send you to France. And if
I do, I can assure you that it will be against my every instinct. I'm under pressure to provide six dog sections at the
end of next week but . . . well, however short we are of men,
I cannot see that it is right to send boys so young."

"I can do the job, sir, I can do it as well as any man."

The Colonel was nodding as he knelt. "Yes," he said quietly. "Yes, I know you can." He reached to stroke Bones.
"My son loved dogs. He too was a fine boy . . . They told me
afterwards that he went over the top and on forward. When
he lost his companions, still he went forward. As he was

bringing prisoners home, he was hit by his own shells . . . Falling short, they told me."

Stanley was defeated, silenced by the Colonel's raw, open grief.

"He, too, was so very young, Stanley."

7 March 1918

Shoeburyness, Essex

Once again Stanley walked up and down Shoeburyness High Street. Two hours every afternoon, for four weeks, he thought, while other men rest or swim in the estuary. How much point is there when we might be stuck here forever? The Colonel is protecting me, he thought, but I have only a brother, and that brother is in France, and France is where I should be.

Still, it was good to be out in the sun with Bones, and they'd made steady progress. Bones rarely showed aggression or suspicion, so far today hadn't growled once.

Stanley's thoughts turned to Thornley. Had anyone worried where he was? What had Miss Bird done when he'd started missing school? Who did Joe play cards with now? Stanley sighed. Had Da done nothing when he'd found him missing? Did he not care?

No new dogs had arrived, despite the Colonel's calls. If more dogs did come, Stanley would have to spend another six weeks training them, but at least he'd know for sure that he'd get to France. There were four days to go until the next batch of keepers and dogs were to report at Folkestone. There'd be a final Homing Run test tomorrow, after which the Colonel would announce who would be drafted out. Bones would do the test, but for what? Stanley sighed and stopped in front of a newsstand carrying the headline of the *Daily Express,* looking for a distraction from these thoughts.

The peace talks between Germany and Russia had finally been concluded. Germany would have more men, more money, more ammunition than ever before. Where was Tom? What would this mean for Tom?

That night Stanley lay awake in his bunk. Around him, the men who'd been given three dogs each were all asleep. Rain rattled on the iron roof like the rat-a-tat-tat of machine-gun fire.

Listening to the rain, Stanley fell into an unsettled sleep. In his dream, water dripped from the tin roof and collected in dark puddles on the floor. The puddles grew and coalesced and began to rise and fill the hut. The water was rising inside Stanley. He couldn't speak and he couldn't breathe because the water was in his throat and he was drowning, while above him danced fragments of golden straw. He reached upward through the raven water to them, but his fingers grasped only shreds of sacking.

The next morning the keepers sat in the truck, ready for the Colonel's address.

"Can you hear that?" said someone. The eerie echo of gunfire was drifting on the wind across the narrow sea from the Western Front.

"I can't wait—can you?—for the cavalry, for the beating drums . . ." said Trigger Doyle. Stanley looked at Trigger aghast. He'd never longed for war, didn't like to think of one man killing another. France was no more and no less to Stanley than the land where Tom was and Da wasn't.

Trigger looked at Stanley expectantly. "Not one for a natter, are you, Stanley Ryder?" But he didn't wait for an answer and shrugged his shoulders. "'S all right. We'll stick together, you and I, and I'll do the talking." Trigger saw it as his job, perhaps, to jolly Stanley along and he never seemed to mind that Stanley didn't say much.

Bones was good at the Homing Run, fast and with iron stamina. Each afternoon of the last three weeks the dogs had been taken by the Colonel's orderlies a distance away from their keepers and had had to find their way back alone over ground they didn't know. First they'd been led away on foot, then in automobiles. Now, for the first time, they were to be taken off in a closed box trailed behind the car. At their destination the orderlies would unload them, put a message giving the time of release into their cylinders, slip their collars, and instruct the dogs to get on.

The Colonel began to speak. "The safe arrival of a message from the back line to the front, or the front to the back, can mean the success or failure of an offensive. Telephone lines can be easily tapped. Wireless communication can be tuned into. A dog, unlike a pigeon, can work at night, in fog, in rain, can swim across a river or a canal or a shell hole. Using a dog as messenger can prevent the tragic and unnecessary death of a human runner. That is why the homing skill has been at the heart of all our training here and today we'll see which dogs are ready for this most dangerous and vital duty."

The dogs were driven away. The keepers moved toward their posts. The light changed minute by minute as clouds scudded across the vast mackerel sky. Stanley buttoned his greatcoat to the neck, stamped his feet, and blew on his hands, his eyes trained on the horizon and a distant church spire. He could see all the arable land between this estuary and the next. Bones would be eight miles away by now, there, below the church spire. At exactly three o'clock he'd be released. Kennel staff were scattered along the route, ready to watch each dog's self-control, ability to avoid temptations, to navigate traffic. The Colonel himself would be watching from a sort of raised hide on the salt marsh, so he could see as much of the course as possible.

Stanley checked his watch. Three ten. They'd come into sight any minute, the faster ones first, then the rest in dribs and drabs.

Even when Bones had been taken farther away, had to cross higher gates, wider dykes, denser barbed wire, still he'd come back, not taking the road he'd traveled outward, but in a beeline. Yes, Bones was good at homing, but this run would include the Firing Drill, the test he'd found so difficult. Still, Stanley said to himself, it made no difference really, if Bones did well or not.

The minutes inched past. Stanley anxiously scuffed the broad flat leaves of the cord grass at his feet. There, almost beneath his left boot, was the spotty head of a dotted chestnut moth. That was the first dotted chestnut of the year. Stanley beckoned to Trigger. Trigger liked moths too. Chestnuts didn't like the cold but now it was warmer. The catkins,

Stanley was thinking now, might be out on the hazel at Thornley.

Through his binoculars, Stanley could see the first dogs—there!—pouring like rolling surf through the narrow gate on to the railway track. In a wave, breath held, as tense as if it were Derby day and their shirts staked on the outcome, the keepers abandoned their cigarettes and their chatter and pressed their field glasses to their eyes. Birdie was setting fire to the bales. The dogs were clambering on to the bank of the watercourse that bounded this side of the village. That was one dog there—now on the far side of the first field—Bones—his height so distinctive—hurling himself into the water. Stanley pictured him disappearing in the current, surfacing, spluttering, head just above the water, muscular legs scrabbling in the froth.

There he was, the first up on the near bank by the coppiced elm, kingly and calm, loping easily toward the wires which stretched, five high and each a foot apart, across the belly of the field. The two largest dogs, Bones and Trigger's dog Gypsy, were level-pegging it toward the wires—No!—Bones was a nose ahead—enough to make a man burst with pride—now soaring the wires in a swift, smooth stream. Stanley felt a vaulting rush of joy as the pack, all shapes and sizes, breeds and colors, ages and abilities, raced for the field gate, now onward to the hurdles, snouts raised like pointers after game. Bones jumped the first hurdle, and the next, and the next with increasing height and ease.

Flames leaped from the top of Birdie's bales, danced around the edges. Smoke rolled and billowed out. It was becoming difficult to see but there at the front of the pack was Bones—pausing—head tilted indignantly at the smoke—now flying into the smog—appearing—a gold-brown streak, on this side. He was so fast—airborne, sailing, floating—four legs off the ground, on, off, the astonishing reach of his forelegs striking the ground so far in front of his nose.

The dogs had reached the broken marshland, the worst lay ahead. There in the marshland, concealed in the reed and the sedge, lay the ambush, the line of firing infantry with their rifles and the kennel men with their mortars. Bones and Gypsy were nose to nose again—no, now Bones was ahead, fiercer in his longing to come home. Trigger was forgetting himself, waving his cap, woolly black hair flying, pink-faced with shouting. The guns burst into a shattering blizzard of fire and noise. Sparks flew. Swelling puffs of black and grey smoke billowed out. Acrid fumes dispersed on the breeze. What would Bones do? Would he come straight through the storm of blanks?

There he was—he'd pulled up mid-gallop the instant the guns had opened fire. The rest of the field surged past in a frothy torrent. Still Bones hesitated, with that familiar, considering-my-options pitch to his head.

"No, Bones. Straight through. Straight on. Just go straight on."

Bones half turned from the guns. Trigger was jumping up and down, victory within his reach. Stanley bit his lip and breathed, "Come, Bones, come. Straight to me. Come straight through."

Bones took a step forward and stopped. He took another step and stopped.

"Come, Bones, come."

Bones was pawing the ground. He raised his head at the guns and barked, then loped forward a couple of easy paces, more like a thoroughbred horse in a show ring than a dog. He drew up, surely, now very close to the guns, lowered his head, lifted his tail, and moved into a long striding run.

"Come, Bones, come, boy, come."

The dog disappeared from view.

"Come, boy, come."

Where was he? Stanley's eyes ached from the strain of trying to see.

There! He'd done it—he'd gone through the firing line, was gathering speed, making time on the dogs at the front, racing with every fiber in his body, jaws set, legs converging, long striding gait the very image of purpose and intent, near the front now, a flurry of dogs in his wake. Trigger was caught off balance as Gypsy hurled himself at his master in a frenzied muddle of tail and leg and tongue. Bones vaulted forward, and Stanley was on his knees, head against the striped velvet coat, arm around the muscular neck.

"Good boy," Stanley whispered. Bones pulled himself free, shook himself, scattering sunlit spray like diamond confetti, then remembering his duty he assembled himself into an untidy sitting position, hind legs awry and sprawling, flanks heaving. Breathless and panting, he lifted his head for the cylinder to be opened.

"Good boy," said Stanley, bursting with pride for this ferocious and graceful animal, for this animal that was loyal beyond all imagining.

"Keeper Ryder." Stanley jumped at the Colonel's voice.

The Colonel was smiling as he addressed Stanley but his words were hard to hear beneath the babel of barking dogs. "He did it your way because he wanted to be with you. You conquered his natural instinct and guided him home."

Seized by sudden and violent indignation, that Bones should have come so far, yet all to no purpose, Stanley stepped forward, only to be intercepted by the Colonel.

"I never wanted to send you forward, Ryder, never thought you should go to France . . . couldn't bring myself to . . . but I've no choice. You are needed, your dog is needed. Even with only one dog, you must go."

Stanley fell to his knees, his cheek to Bones's giant muzzle.

"Bones," he whispered. "Bones, do you hear?"

The Colonel shook his head sadly, fondly, as he looked on. "You've done well, Ryder, very well. Bones has taken your courage, your sense of honor for his own. He'll always be true, faithful, and brave, even to the last beat of his heart, would—I've no doubt—give his own life for you." The Colonel pondered, scrutinizing Stanley. "Whatever lies ahead for you both, remember that to him, you are all his life."

With a gentle, paternal shake of his head, he turned and walked away.

9 March 1918

Folkestone

At Folkestone the keepers took a narrow path down the cliffs. Below them on the water sat a white-painted hospital ship, a grey-painted steamer, and beyond them, a destroyer and her escort. Stanley eyed the waiting steamer. That would be his ship, ready for her dash across the Channel. Once aboard, he thought, as he stood aside for a group of soldiers climbing upward, there'd be no turning back. With a shock, Stanley saw the lean, drawn faces and sloppy dress of the soldiers and he heard their jeers.

"Shiny and new . . . but not for long."

"Just boys—the Hun'll go through this lot like a hot knife through butter."

Stanley placed a reassuring hand on Bones's head as another laughed, "Dogs this week, they'll be sending the women next . . ."

Stanley looked at his own greatcoat, buttoned to the throat, at his immaculate boots and puttees, at the blue and white armlet on his elbow, the crossed flags on his cuff. The dribble of gaunt, skin-and-bone men pushed on past. Did all returning soldiers look like this? Stanley chewed his lips watching, beginning, for the first time, to wonder what lay ahead for him and Bones.

They boarded the SS *Victoria* and Stanley squeezed himself into the last square inches left on deck. Bones leaned heavily into Stanley's left side. Like an overlarge child, Bones always sat as close as possible to Stanley, preferably partially on top of him, Bones's slobbery jaws settling comfortably on Stanley's arm.

Stanley watched the searchlights playing along the English coast as the SS *Victoria* took him from all that he'd ever known, across the sea for the first time in his life, to he knew not what. The torpedo boats that flanked either side of the *Victoria* were there to protect her from the invisible enemy, the German submarines that might be stalking the black water beneath her. Somewhere on that dark coast behind Stanley was Thornley, somewhere there would be Da in his red chair, Da with Rocket at his feet. Stanley felt not homesickness but loss. In spite of everything, if he could, he might, at that second, have flung himself into the treacherous water, swum for home, and made one last attempt to recover the father he'd lost.

He shivered and pulled the collar of his greatcoat closer around his neck, gazing out on to the black water. Growing eddies of anxiety for what lay ahead rolled aside Stanley's grief for what lay behind until he fell, finally, into an uneasy sleep.

Just before dawn the SS *Victoria* dropped anchor at Le Havre. The men disembarked in dark and drizzle, amid the shouts and curses of officers. Stanley and Bones took their place in the line of men that felt its way around immense stacks of military goods, mules, and ammunition dumps that packed the wharf.

Beyond the wharf, in an open space lit with lanterns, guides and NCOs shouted out the names of different regiments, "Loyal North Lancs on the right!" "King's Liverpool on the left!" Stanley's unit shuffled into line with the Royal Engineers. He and Trigger were under orders to report to Central Kennels HQ when they arrived at Etaples. Street hawkers circled while they waited, selling sweets and cigarettes.

As dawn broke, a troop of wounded passed, heading for the wharf. They all looked the same in the anxious half-light, all grey-faced and mud-splattered. In the depths of their staring eyes, Stanley caught something of the horrors they'd seen. He remembered the line in Tom's card—"the world will never be the same again for those of us here." No, Stanley thought, defiant, it won't: the world will never be the same for me, anyway, not only because of what lies ahead, but because of what lies behind. Because of what Da did, nothing will ever be the same again.

However, as the wounded men tramped away, Stanley's defiance ebbed as he realized that he'd never thought about war close up. He hadn't come to France for honor or glory, for love of England, for hatred of Germany, but only to be with Tom.

Stanley and Bones were crammed into a corner of a pitch-dark cattle truck labeled in large black letters "8 CHEVAUX ou 40 HOMMES." The train clanked along at walking pace. When it made yet another of its endless, unexplained stops, the doors slammed open to admit more men. Stanley would eat something, now, while there was light to see by. He peeled open his ration of canned beef. The blood red of the canned beef shocked and disconcerted him. His hunger evaporated. The doors banged shut and Stanley sat in the dark again, reassured by the solid bulk of Bones, for the smell of him, for his warmth, and for the comfortable, easy manner in which he took each new movement forward.

Stanley's thoughts turned to Tom and, more practically now, how to find him. Tom would be so surprised to see his little brother in France, in uniform, a keeper with a beautiful dog and a vital job to do.

The train clanged and clanked onward, and as the scale of the war began to dawn on Stanley, he began to accept that perhaps he'd not be fighting alongside Tom, that they might be miles and miles from each other. Tom was in the East Lancashires, but with which corps? Stanley had never asked and now must find out without drawing attention to himself, mustn't look like a young boy trying to find his big brother.

"Pick 'em up. Left-right, left-right."

Regulation marching pace was two and a half miles an hour. Stanley's misgivings about finding Tom grew as they proceeded onward over dazzling white sand toward what looked like a city of tents and hutments. He looked aghast at the vast and dreadful encampment, sickened by its thick stench of stale food. They passed tents, tents, and more tents.

When they reached GHQ Central Kennels, Bones was

led away by an orderly to an enclosed area with rows of kennels. Feeling bereft, Stanley made his way, numb with exhaustion, to the bell-tent he and fifteen other men had been assigned.

Just before he fell asleep that night he heard the sound of gunfire and Trigger Doyle whispered knowingly, "Guns. You always hear them when the wind blows from the east."

"How many men are here at Etaples?"

"Ten thousand, I've heard, and growing every day. They're packing us in. The Hun is up to something and Haig is getting ready."

Trigger's pride and excitement were so at odds with Stanley's misgivings.

Ten thousand. How would he find Tom? There was something, Stanley remembered, called Cross Post, a mail service operated by the Army. Was the Cross Post censored? he wondered, suspecting that it might be. When Tom replied to Stanley, he'd almost certainly say his little brother was too young and must go home, so that when the letter was read by the Censor, the officials would be alerted and would send Stanley back.

Every instinct for survival made him steer clear of the official channels. He could ask Trigger, perhaps, what Trigger would do, but he distrusted Trigger's judgement. If he were sent back home, he had nowhere to go, and he'd have to leave Bones, as Army property, behind.

No, writing to Tom using the Cross Post was too dangerous. Tom would make sure to get Stanley sent home. Stanley would have to find out where Tom's unit was and then, only when he was face to face with Tom, would he explain.

Etaples was more brutal than Chatham, more brutal than anything Stanley had ever known. Everything had to be done on the double, everyone shouted all the time. After just one week he was tense and tired, enervated by the constant noise and dust.

He was lined up in alphabetical order in front of the Sergeant-Major for Pay Parade. It was tiresome being an "R" because it could take an hour till the Sergeant-Major got to you.

Stanley's thoughts had turned to finding Tom, when Rigby, the "R" in line before himself, whispered, "They say we've been lucky it's been quiet so far but that it's going to change. The quiet only means Ludendorff's up to no good, he's busy resupplying his troops . . . put six new divisions on the Amiens front."

Everyone knew that the German General, Ludendorff, was hauling his big guns up closer to the city of Amiens. Ludendorff had to take Amiens before he could strike at Paris. None of this really mattered to Stanley so he smiled back at Rigby. Tom mattered and Bones mattered, so he was only half listening, half thinking of what he'd buy with his pay. He and Trigger might go this afternoon to the YMCA hut and buy chocolate and tins of apricots, then run with their dogs to the farmhouse where they sold loaves of bread a yard long, all hot and soft and crusty.

Stanley stepped up to the table, saluted and held out his left hand. Etaples was full of silly regulations—and it had to be your left hand to receive your pay.

He and Trigger threaded their way to the YMCA between

tents and vehicles and the crowds of villagers who came up on Sundays. Small French boys tugged at them, pestering, hawking dictionaries, spearmint, and grapes. They circumnavigated a truck, behind which knelt a priest in front of a packing case. Rows of men knelt on the ground between boxes of ammunition, which served as pews. They'd be about to go up to the Front. All men were offered Communion before going up the line.

Stanley caught sight of the priest's boots. Sticking out of the bottom of his surplice, they had shiny spurs on them. A horseman. A idea struck Stanley: he could ask the priest.

Trigger was laughing. "Taking Communion'll be enough to make them jumpy if they're not already."

A priest would be discreet; Stanley would be safe with him. A soldier at the back of the congregation, seeing the boys hovering and thinking they wanted to worship, rose and handed Stanley an Order of Service. Father Bill Loveday, it said, was taking the Mass.

"Thank you," said Stanley. "Don't wait for me," he told Trigger. He'd wait till Communion was over, then he'd approach Bill Loveday of the shiny spurs. It was because he was both a churchman and a horseman that Stanley felt comfortable about asking him how to find Tom.

"Suit yourself," said Trigger.

Stanley knelt and waited.

The following afternoon Stanley waited in the Bull Ring, as the exercise arena was known. There were anything up to five thousand men exercising in this vast ring at any time, so it could be a long wait till his unit was called to march out. Bones was too hot, his flanks heaving, his tongue lolling, his solid bulk tiring more easily than other dogs.

Idly, Stanley watched an infantry unit on bayonet drill. A straw-filled dummy in a Hun helmet hung from a post. An officer was yelling "Kill the bastard!" as the men ran at it with fixed bayonets. It made Stanley feel uncomfortable watching, and it made him wonder about Tom. Did Tom smile as he steadied his hand and prepared to fire? How many men had Tom killed? What did it feel like to kill a man?

He'd heard nothing from the priest since their conversation. Father Bill had said to Stanley that he'd be going straight from that Communion up to the Front, but that when he came out again he'd make enquiries.

Bones pricked his ears and picked up his pace as they neared the friendly crossed flags that announced Central Kennels, and made their way to the bomb pits. Bones knew it was feeding time but he didn't worry himself, as Stanley did, about the ready availability of so much fresh horsemeat. Each day at feeding time he'd think of the Thornley horses and worry for them, wonder how they'd fared and whether Lord Chorley still thought it was a fine thing for a horse to go to war. Each day, too, it made Stanley glad that Da would never see the bomb pits.

Two days later, Stanley and Trigger stood in line for breakfast. There'd still been nothing from Father Bill of the shiny spurs. Stanley reached the front of the line and took a tin of tea from the first hut, from the second a lump of bread dipped in bacon fat. He was glad of the bacon fat; the bread was softer after a dunking.

"Come on, Bones," said Stanley, his mouth still full of bread. He'd seen the excited huddle of Royal Engineers around the Post Office.

"Just walk on past. There'll be no mail for us." It wasn't that Stanley worried about Bones growling any more, it was just less painful if Stanley didn't hope that someone might ever write to him. Having Bones was better probably than having parcels or people to write to. Stanley and Trigger always walked straight past the Post Office. It was an unspoken understanding between them.

"Ryder! Ryder!"

Stanley's heart raced. Trigger's head shot around, amusement and curiosity in his eyes. That shout had come from near the Post Office, from Rigby. Rigby would know if Stanley had a letter because they were alphabetically close. Stanley turned and dragged the confused Bones back to the mail orderly, his fists growing clammy and hot. Bones was hanging back, reproach in his eyes, disliking any variation to his routine.

Stanley must look calm, mustn't look alarmed. It wouldn't be from Da or Tom, just from Father Bill, probably, writing to say where Tom was.

"It won't bite. It's only a parcel," the mail orderly said, holding out a brown paper package. Stanley composed himself. A parcel. Not Father Bill then.

He walked, puzzling, toward the kennels. The parcel was quite heavy and medium-sized. Stamped "APO S11." That would be the Etaples Post Office stamp. "ON ACTIVE SERVICE" was stamped across the top of the parcel, giving Stanley a little hug of pride, despite his anxiety. "PASSED

BY 2959 CENSOR" was stamped above that. There was something familiar about the writing but Stanley couldn't identify what. A parcel, he thought, though, was a good sign. If it were bad news, it would be a letter, not a parcel.

Stanley began to run to Bones's kennel. He sank down behind it. The dog settled himself on Stanley's feet. Stanley tore open the parcel. Bones showed a playful interest in the shredded paper wrapper and a look of disdain for its contents. Five buns wrapped in brown paper. Beneath them, something else, heavier. A jar of honey. This small tenderness after so many lonely, brutal months left Stanley helpless. Only Stanley's Biology teacher had searched for him—she'd found out where he was and she'd sent honey. Stanley's thoughts, though, weren't with Lara Bird: they were with Da. Why, when his own Da had done nothing?

Bones looked with disdain at the honey, with interest at the buns, with concern at his master, all three emotions so clear in those expressive eyes.

Miss Bird knew where Stanley was, and she wasn't cross or she wouldn't have sent the parcel. Had she told Da? There must be a letter in there too. Stanley scrabbled through the newspaper. There it was, at the bottom. And something else: a pack of cards. Those would be from Joe. Stanley looked at Bones, holding the paper up. In that folded paper lay their fate.

"What do you say, Bones? Shall we open it?" Bones hoped Stanley was talking about the buns and dipped his head a little closer towards them.

Nethercott, Longridge

17 March 1918

Dear Stanley,

I've been so worried about you. I guessed
what you'd done that first morning you
didn't come to school and I went straight
to Thornley. Your Da would say nothing, but
your note was on his lap and he handed it
to me, shaking his head again and again, but
saying nothing. I read your note, and know
what happened, how shocked and upset you
must have been. I understand why you've
gone, why you won't come home and live
alone again with your father. Because of this,
it's taken me a while to trace you as I have
been careful not to reveal anything or raise
any concerns during my search.

Stanley's shoulders fell with relief.

But Stanley, this morning, your father appeared at Nethercott asking me to look after Rocket. He was anxious and paced to and fro - looked as though he'd neither slept nor eaten for some time. I don't know what he plans to do nor why he left Rocket with me, but I am sure he means to find you and to make you return.

I have not yet told Tom where you are - while he is in the trenches, I don't want him to have any more worry than he must already have, but he'll be home next week. I will have to tell him then that I know where you are and I know how scared he will be for you.

Tom on leave next week? Stanley whipped the paper over to check the date. Written on the 17th—it was the 20th today. Tom might be at Thornley now—wouldn't be back in France for at least two weeks. By then Stanley himself would be at the Front. It was all wrong, all topsy-turvy—Tom in England, Stanley in France. It would be Lara Bird who'd tell Tom where Stanley was, not himself. What would she say? What would Tom do? In turmoil, Stanley read on:

Colonel Richardson tells me that your work is in the Signals Service and is mainly behind the lines. He wrote how glad he was to hear from someone in connection with you, and said you have a great gift with animals. He said that he sent you to France with only one dog to make it unlikely you'd be sent to areas of the greatest danger where more dogs would be required.

Stanley, it is better that you should return of your own accord than that your father or brother should force you to. The trenches are no place for you, Stanley, and I pray you

will come to me at Nethercott. Please write to
me to say you will come and live with me
I should like, above all, to tell Tom you will
come so that the leave- for which he has
waited so long- is not spoilt.

I know your father has not always been
kind to you, that he has done a violent and
unnatural thing, for which now you feel you
can never forgive him, but in time, I think,
you will understand what grief can do to a
man. Until then you must remember how
much your father has lost already, that he _is_
still your father, that he loves you dearly and
as dearly would love you to return.

God bless and keep you safe and bring
you home to us,
Lara Bird.

Stanley's fingers found his pocket and curled around the
Bryant & May matchbox. He flipped the matchbox over
and over as he revolved all the possible outcomes of what
Lara Bird would tell Tom. Yes, he thought; yes, Tom will
understand I couldn't stay at home after what Da did. Stan-

ley revolved the matchbox faster. Yes, Tom would see, Tom would understand.

Stanley's fingers slowed to a standstill. Live at Nethercott? Agitation about Tom's reaction was replaced by anger. If Da wanted Stanley back, why hadn't he done something? Why had it been left to his teacher to look for him? Stanley flipped the matchbox again, faster and faster. Da had never come to Chatham or Shoeburyness or Etaples; there'd been nothing, not a sound from him. Da had never come to find his son, so what was he planning on doing when he left Rocket with Lara Bird?

It would be easy to creep home, to slip back into school life, to live at Nethercott. Stanley could get out of the Army because of his age—that was his trump card; but it wouldn't help Bones. Bones was Army property and it would be a criminal offense to take him away. No, there could be no going back, whatever Tom or Lara Bird said.

"Oh, Bones! What do I do?" Stanley looked up toward the buzzing of the British planes dodging over the German lines. Breaths of fleecy smoke puffed up around the planes, clouds of white, green, and yellow in the azure sky.

Bones settled his wet snout on Stanley's lap. It would be a relief to go back to school, to live at Nethercott. But Bones? No. Bones belonged to him and he belonged to Bones. Whatever they'd got themselves into, they were in it together.

21 March 1918

Etaples

As Stanley walked toward Central Kennels, Trigger came running up, excited and breathless, thrusting yesterday's *Daily Express* into Stanley's hands:

50 MILES OF OUR LINE ATTACKED
ON A VASTER SCALE THAN EVER BEFORE

"Four thousand enemy guns, a hurricane bombardment, Stanley. The Hun wants Paris, that's what all this is about. Look, he's got tanks now and more men, more money, more ammunition. Something's up—that's why we're being summoned." Trigger's enthusiasm for action and beating drums never faltered, Stanley was thinking, even if the enemy had more tanks and money and men than the English.

The news from the Front had grown worse each day. More and more officers had applied to the Kennels for dogs but still there'd been no fresh dogs sent out. At Central Kennels, there was an air of quiet desperation.

The Kennel Staff were hurriedly organizing and rearranging the keepers into units, and the units into bigger platoons.

"Doyle, Rigby, Ryder. Together you form a Dog Unit reporting to the Second Battalion of the Devons, Twenty-Third Brigade of the Eighteenth Division, Fourteenth Corps. You're under orders to make ready to go forward by rail at dawn tomorrow. For administrative purposes only, you're attached to a formation of the Royal Engineers."

"Second to none," said Trigger, beaming, as they paraded at the Orderly Room for an issue of blue and white armlets. "The Eighteenth are second to none. We're lucky, Stanley."

They moved on to the Quarter-Master's stores where Stanley, without enthusiasm, collected his "small kit," a blanket and groundsheet, which could also be a raincoat as it had a collar at one side down the middle.

That evening the news grew worse. The Germans had begun an advance on Amiens. Amiens was the gateway to Paris, a railroad and communications center, which the Hun needed if he wanted the capital. This morning, too, they'd fired a gun, they called it the Paris Gun, which had a range of over eighty-one miles. They'd fired at fifteen-minute intervals all day, with the first shell landing at seven in the morning, right on the bank of the Seine.

Stanley lay in bed, half listening to the morose, fearful talk of the men in his tent. The name of a particular village, Villers-Bretonneux, kept coming up. Only nine miles from Amiens, Villers had been right in the middle of the line of attack. The attack had been devastating, men said, but the line had held.

"Ludendorff will hit out again now, any minute now . . . wants to do it before more Americans arrive . . . He's nervous about the Americans."

"They'll send us up there. That's where we'll be going tomorrow, to the Villers sector."

The gunfire sounded closer than ever before. At the foot of Stanley's mattress lay two gas helmets, goggles, a steel helmet, and one hundred and twenty rounds of ammunition. Why did the Army waste ammunition on someone in the back lines, attached only to a Signal Station? Stanley wondered. The sinister-looking gas masks—his and Bones's—were twin ghouls gaping at him. Why was there such urgency? Why had they had to turn in with their boots on, and their puttees laced?

What on earth was he doing? While Tom was in England, why was Stanley going into battle to defend Villers, Amiens, Paris? Why?

Stanley and his unit, and their dogs, marched along a broad, poplar-lined road, listening to the raucous singing of the cooks behind them, smelling sweat and smoke, hearing the ring of boots on cobbles. The whole world seemed to be moving east, a continuous stream of horses, troops, and ammunition carts. Only the ambulances traveled both ways, fleets of them coming and going. There was an endless supply out here of both ambulances and horseflesh.

They marched through a village called Aubigny, another called Fouilloy. Stanley fought the pain of the aching muscles of his neck beneath the steel helmet, fought the blisters on his tendons where the laces of his boots dug in, the calluses on his heels, but the dogs were curious and easy and cheerful.

They passed an abandoned village, its streets strewn with

sewing machines, mangles, bicycles, pots and pans and china. Trigger had grown silent, his enthusiasm for beating drums now on the wane. A cluster of crosses stood, huddled and gaunt, at an intersection in the road. Despite the heat, Stanley shivered. With each passing moment, with each passing sight, his fear grew.

Beyond the crosses and the ruined houses, one last house straggled some way behind the others. Each front room gaped, as open as a doll's house, its facade completely gone. Where was the child who used to push that wicker baby carriage? At the foot of the stone steps to the house, indifferent to the clouds of dust, indifferent to the passing traffic, sat an old man, holding his head in his hands.

That white hair was so like Da's. The ground was giving way beneath Stanley, all his certainties in flight. His own father, so many miles away, might be sitting like that, his white head in his hands. Bones pulled at the lead, but still Stanley craned his neck to stare. The man's head rose, leaden with pain. Stanley started as though he'd seen a ghost.

"Oh God," he said. "What have I done?"

The old man started forward, arms outstretched, then faltered and stood for a few heartbreaking seconds, his trembling hands hovering in the empty air. He sank down again, his hands over his eyes.

Bones tugged again at the lead. On Stanley marched, like a sleepwalker through a chamber of horrors, between wooden crosses, around or over the carcasses of horses, onward past a sign, adrift in a pile of rubble all overgrown with wild mustard. That rubble, scarcely one brick on top of another now, had once been a village, and that sign had once named it. Haunted still by that lonely white head, Stanley passed more ruined houses, ruined lives, ruined families, growing more troubled at each step by the idea that he'd perhaps done wrong to his own.

Another fifty minutes passed. The column halted and men drank from their bottles. By the side of the road lay birdcages, dolls, baby carriages, cots, and bed frames. Bones collapsed, his flanks heaving at Stanley's feet, and placed his muzzle on Stanley's boots. Trigger kicked the ground.

"Hammered into dust . . . The fighting here must've been yard by yard . . . whole villages just hammered into dust."

Stanley poured Bones some water, listening to Rigby and Doyle, seeing a fleeting, troubled frown cross Trigger's clear forehead, his voice unusually subdued.

"They say it was a rough time . . . all hands on deck . . . just a desperate hodgepodge making up the line—bottlewashers, cooks, artillery drivers . . ."

Stanley's fear for what lay ahead grew. He placed a hand on Bones's head. "All hands on deck" would mean dog keepers too. Would he, after all, end up in the front line? He and Bones? A fleet of ambulances passed, sending up clouds of choking dust.

Trigger's voice was still subdued. "They're from Villers, these Tin Lizzies . . . all from Villers."

"They've had a hot time there," said Rigby. "All because of Paris. If the Hun gets Amiens he can range all his guns on Paris."

"They say he's going to have another crack at Villers," said Trigger. "Ludendorff's going to attack again. That's why we're going up . . . Haig's sending us all up there to save Amiens."

When the dust cleared, Stanley noticed amid a row of ruined buildings opposite, a bar and a sign still standing: "THE ESTAMINET AU CHEVAL NOIR." The inn had no roof or upper floor, but some horses, a team of gunners perhaps, were stabled in the ground-floor rooms. Though the buildings on either side were razed to the ground, there, amid a scene of desolation and destruction, the horses stood, as dozy and peaceful as in the green fields of home.

The support lines lay across undulating land, above a low-lying plain intersected by canals and ringed on all sides by low, wooded hills. The line stopped. Stanley's unit was met by their guide, an infantryman of the Devons. The infantryman looked a little put out, a little alarmed by Bones, and made sure to keep a good distance between himself and the dog as the guide ordered them not to smoke and not to talk. In silence and in single file they dropped into a deep communication trench leading to the back lines.

The air was thick, and hot, and stale. Curiosity getting the better now of his anxiety, Stanley admired the camouflage cover overhead, wire netting threaded with real grass, and the deep clay walls of the trench. He thought of the man-hours of digging that had gone into the making of the trench and felt glad not to be burrowing with the Engineers. Bones was large and clumsy, a giant in these cramped proportions, and the men hauling provisions up and down the trench cursed him as they passed.

They took a narrower access branch, which emerged into the back lines. More guides were waiting at an intersection to take companies up to their front-line posts. In absolute silence, Stanley and Bones, Doyle, Rigby, and their dogs, and a Regimental Signaler with a pair of flags stuck in his pack, followed the dusty, claustrophobic, right-angled zigzagging of the trench for perhaps a mile. The straight bits, known as "bays," were crowded with men, some leaning against the sandbag walls, smoking and looking bored. Others sat on gas cans playing cards or reading. One man stretched out a hand to Bones. That wasn't good: Bones would be distracted from his work if he was petted or offered food. Surely the infantry had been warned not to give the dogs food?

"No," said Stanley firmly, a little surprised at himself. "No petting and no food."

Trigger looked impressed. He was holding up six fingers. He'd developed a habit of counting Stanley's words. Stanley grinned back.

Where Stanley could see over the parapet, the front edge of the trench, there was a clear view in all directions. The back line here ran along a bit of a ridge, overlooking a slope, and below that, the plain was ringed with trees and a river. So this, thought Stanley, this is it. This is the Somme. This terrible plain, slashed with the knife cuts of trenches; this is where Tom fought.

The view was bald and abrupt: first the potato fields, then the slope, the plain, then the German fences and wire. Well behind the line lay the village of Villers-Bretonneux on a spearhead of the plateau, a commanding position astride an old Roman road. It was clear to Stanley why the Hun wanted Villers.

A new guide met Stanley and took him to the back station, Battalion Headquarters, instructing him to report to Corporal Hunter, the officer in command of Signals for the Devons of XIV Corps. They reached a right-angled corner and some narrow wooden steps. Stanley was waved on down the steps, while Doyle and Rigby were to follow on. Trigger put an arm around Stanley, but addressed Bones as he said, "It's up to you now, you'll have to do the talking for him. Look after him. Take care of him." Then to Stanley he said, "Good luck, Stanley."

"Good luck, Trigger."

Stanley and Bones dropped ten feet or so underground, the air growing still thicker and closer, and entered a stuffy chamber lit by dim electric light. Wooden posts supported the ceiling and wooden boards lined the walls. Stanley bowed his head under the low ceiling.

Bones collapsed, panting at Stanley's feet in the narrow entrance. No one turned. There was no noise or movement in the room, the air still with concentration. Signals operators and instrument repairers, wearing headphones and the brassards of the Royal Engineers, sat around a large wireless set. There were lamps for night signals, and a heliograph, the simple, brilliant wireless telegraph that signalled Morse code with flashes of sunlight reflected by a mirror. Beyond this room Stanley glimpsed a smaller chamber, filled with dispatch riders and runners.

Heavy cables were looped around the room and out through the door. At the far end were buzzers and Fuller-phones. Buzzers, Stanley knew from his signaling course at Chatham, were easily intercepted by the enemy, but the

Fuller-phones, a portable signaling device, could be used either down telephone or telegraph lines and were safer. A figure stooped, ears toward an amplifier, eyes on a cable map.

"Corporal Hunter?" ventured Stanley.

The stooping figure by the cable map turned his head, assessed Stanley, then caught sight of Bones. Corporal Hunter shot up, his head, like Stanley's, stopping just short of the low ceiling. They were almost the same height, each eyeing the other with bent necks. The Corporal's eyes whipped down to Bones.

"For the love of God, a dog?" The Corporal grasped a handkerchief and swabbed his brow. "A dog? A dog and a child . . . ?"

Were Stanley and Bones not needed? Did the Corporal not know what dogs were for? Had he not used them in the line? Stanley saw the equipment, all the cables and buzzers and kit that surrounded the Corporal, and felt misgivings, but Bones sat still, proud and waiting for a command.

Hunter lifted the handkerchief from his brow and looked at Bones, again with disbelief. "A schoolboy and his lap-dog . . ."

"The dog's as good as any man, sir, for the job," said Stanley, riled.

Hunter looked at him in surprise, but then, shaking his head with pantomime exasperation, dismissed Stanley with an angry wave of his hand. "Fidget. Take the boy to his bunk."

Fidget? Where? It would be good to be with someone he knew. A huddled figure in the corner unfurled itself into a long narrow shape and drifted toward the door—definitely Fidget: the same tall Fidget with the sister who made fruit cakes, the Fidget Stanley had last seen at Chatham. Stanley started forward but Fidget looked away, circumnavigating Bones with exaggerated caution.

"Creep," hissed Stanley, riled again now, as he stepped into the doorway, pulling Bones with him so that they had Fidget cornered, all of them crowded in the narrow entrance—but wounded, too, that Fidget should be taking his cue from Hunter in this way.

Stanley saluted Hunter and turned, and Bones was in an instant on his feet, setting off with a step so willing you'd never know he'd marched all day. Fidget led them up the steps and along the adjoining thirty yards or so of trench, past servants' dugouts to what was no more than a cavity, scratched into the front wall.

Fidget gave a hesitant grin. "Your bunk, also known as a 'funk-hole.'" He laughed and placed a hand on Stanley's shoulder, rather more friendly now that he was out of Hunter's sight. Stanley shrugged him off.

Two wooden posts supported an iron ceiling. Two hard-board platforms stood one above the other, covered in sandbags. A small shelf held tins of canned beef, a tin of jam, one of café-au-lait, and one of butter, and half a loaf of bread. There was a side shelf with a mirror, matches, candles, and a tin of cigarettes. It was good about the jam, the bread and butter, and perhaps he could trade the canned beef and the cigarettes for something else. Opposite the funk-hole was a ledge cut into the trench wall, two or three feet above the trench floor, which ran all along it, facing the enemy. If you stood on the fire step, you could see over the parapet.

Fidget sat on Stanley's lower platform, on the sandbags, and mocked a sort of bouncing up and down on them. "Cushy," he said, his too-mobile face contorting itself into an expression of alarmed discomfort. He disappeared into the adjoining funk-hole and reappeared clasping a shovel. "You can make it wider."

Fidget was lingering, not hurrying back to Hunter's Signal Station. Stanley felt a wave of distaste for Fidget, was hot and tired, and cross about having to sleep next to the man who'd pretended not to know him. Bones meanwhile, tail tense, was stalking something in Fidget's hole. As Stanley moved to retrieve Bones, he glimpsed the object of Bones's attentions.

"Pigeons?" Stanley spluttered.

"What's the matter with pigeons?" Fidget asked, his expression uncertain, suspended somewhere between pride and hurt at Stanley's scorn. He manoeuvred himself so that he stood between the huge and ferocious Bones and his little pigeon basket. Stanley laughed again, a little uncomfortably now. However ridiculous an animal a pigeon might be, Hunter would be accustomed to using them as message carriers.

Richardson had said that there were over twenty thousand pigeons on active service. Fidget had been grinning rather sheepishly, but now he rallied.

"The Corporal finds my pigeons very reliable. I don't think he sees much need for dogs."

If the dogs hadn't worked in this sector, Stanley was

thinking, the Corporal would probably always use Fidget's pigeons, so Bones would never get a chance.

"A skylark," said Fidget in a conversational tone, peering through the netting roof of the trench, his attention drawn by a loud, liquid chirrup. A bird mounted higher and higher on rapid fluttering wings, describing wide circles in the violet sky. "They eat skylarks. The French eat skylarks."

How little, thought Stanley, he knew of France. He'd never thought much about the French, nor about what they ate. Yet here he was, in line, here to defend the men who ate skylarks.

Fidget hovered behind Stanley, searching for something else to say, and Stanley sensed that he wanted to make amends, knew that he'd been unkind. Fidget had always been odd, remembered Stanley, awkward and changeable, but never meant any harm. Fidget was tapping Stanley's shoulder.

"It's not so bad here once you get used to it, and the Corporal's always rough to anyone new. Come on, I'll make you some tea."

Stanley filled Bones's bowl with water, and was watching the dog slurp when Fidget popped around again. Fidget's sudden, wraithlike apparitions would take some getting used to.

"Half a bleeding hour—and bingo. Lukewarm ditch-water." He handed Stanley a tin of tea, smacking his lips, and swallowing noisily from his own. "Drink it toot-sweet." The surface of the tea was strangely unctuous, but Stanley was thirsty and grateful, and put it to his lips. Fidget laughed as Stanley gagged and spluttered.

"Everything up here tastes of gasoline. All kettles are old gas cans."

Later, at Rations-Up, when Cook handed out McConochie's vegetable stew, it too had the same oily sheen, and when Stanley steeled himself to try it, it was gritty and inedible.

Everything grew quiet and dark, the lights of distant villages bloomed in clusters along the horizon. Stanley lay on his sandbag, in his coat and trench boots, his blanket over him, his kitbag for a pillow, still hungry, listening to the comforting sound of Bones's breathing. Here, less than two miles from the massed weight of the Kaiser's army, it was good to have Bones in his bunk with him. All night men passed to and fro along the trench, each new movement making Stanley jump out of his skin. Stanley rolled over. Sandbags, as well as Fidget's startled spurts of sleep-talk, he thought, would take a bit of getting used to.

Through the netting Stanley saw the huge canopy of stars and felt the crisp night air on his face. If only Tom would write. He'd surely write once Lara Bird told him everything. She'd have told him everything by now. Whatever Tom might do about Stanley's having enlisted, it would still be good to hear from him; to hear, too, how Da was. Perhaps Lara Bird would write again soon, to tell him that she'd seen Da, that he was all right. How often, he wondered, could you expect a Biology teacher to write to you? Perhaps too, if she wrote, she'd send something else to eat.

Bones whickered in his sleep. Stanley grinned to himself, thinking that Bones might be dreaming of plovers or of Fidget's pigeons. It would be a job keeping Bones off those pigeons. "True, faithful, and brave, even to the last beat of his heart," Colonel Richardson had said. Stanley knew then, as he mouthed these words, that however much he wanted to see Tom, he had a duty to Bones, too; that he must be true and faithful; and that whatever Tom wanted his little brother to do, Stanley would stay with Bones. And if they got a chance, they'd show Corporal Hunter—they'd show him what they could do.

31 March 1918

A few miles to the east of Villers-Bretonneux

Lying at the full extent of his lead, Bones's muzzle twitched with playful menace, every nerve in his giant frame taut. No bigger than a ping-pong ball, a field mouse was tapping on a dry leaf with a forepaw. Stanley tightened his grip on the lead, feeling a neighborly affection for this plucky, unknowing creature. In every crevice of this sinister land lay enough steel to throw the earth's bowels to the sky, to cast the tiny mouse a thousand feet high.

"No," said Stanley again, to warn Bones off the field mouse. He, Keeper Ryder, of the 2nd Devons, of the 18th Division, had had nothing better to do, for eight whole days, than watch Bones patrol a field mouse. Bones liked to divide his attentions between the mouse and the pigeon basket. Corporal Hunter liked his Fuller-phone, and he liked pigeons, and he saw no point at all in dogs.

In the afternoons Stanley would play rummy with Fidget. They used the playing cards Joe had sent, and that pack made Stanley miss Joe every time he saw it, but he'd won yesterday. His luck, at cards at least, had held from Longridge to the Somme. Fidget might have the pigeons Hunter found so useful, but Stanley always had the best hand.

Stanley rose to get Bones's brush. Bones leaped up, forgetting the mouse. He responded to Stanley's every movement, even to the movement of his little finger, in case it were a sign that he was needed. His readiness—eagerness—to be sent, did his master require it, even to the ends of the earth, made Stanley's heart ache. If only the Corporal would give them a chance.

Stanley glanced over the parapet as he rose. A magpie was loitering in the weeds immediately ahead, his lurid coat iridescent and gross in the arid glare of the sun, a malevolent gleam in its carnivorous eye. Each day had been hotter and whiter than the day before, the plain more menacing, more foreboding with each passing hour, as the two enemies watched one another, each dreading the assault they knew would come but neither knowing when. By day the plain was so still, while by night men scrambled over it like badgers, burrowing, tunneling, laying cables.

That plain was drained of color in the glare of the sun. No hedgerows. No thrushes, no leaves, no trees. Only magpies. Magpies and bluebottles. Both as lurid, as gluttonous as each other. This was a funny sort of place to fight over. Not like the hills and sudden clefts and ancient walls of Longridge. Longridge was country worth fighting for.

Each brush stroke sent up a cloud of grey dust. When Bones was clean, his yellow stripes shone like gold. Stanley blinked away the dust in his eyes and began to trim the fur between Bones's paws, while Bones lay prostrate, purring, his neck and head straining mousewards. Stanley waved his scissors at a cloud of midges. If it wasn't the flies that bothered you here, it was the midges. Or it was Fidget. Fidget, always there, on his fire step, always ready to regale them with some bad news. Trigger would have been better company. Stanley wondered if his dogs were being used.

He wiped the sweat from his brow.

"It's too quiet, altogether too quiet," said Fidget, blowing a smoke ring from his Woodbine into the camouflage netting. "I don't like the quiet. It means it'll be coming any minute now, Stanley, the attack on this front. We've got nineteen infantry divisions, and he"—Fidget waved his Woodbine in the direction of the enemy—"he's got sixty-four. He shelled Paris again, did you hear, on Palm Sunday, and again on Good Friday. They were in church, Stanley, on their knees in prayer, when they died."

It was best to ignore Fidget and his doomsaying, his rumor-mongering, though Stanley noticed that the infantry did listen to Fidget. In the Signals Service you knew much more than the infantry who were never told anything, so Fidget's words were repeated like Chinese whispers up and down the line. Rumors were traded at rations time, gaining currency with each repetition, and most of them were started by Fidget.

"Today, Fritz is busy south of the railway line. Pushed the French back, pushing us back. But here—he's too quiet in this sector. It's going to be bad, Stanley, that's why Haig's sending more troops, Australians, New Zealanders, whatever he can get his hands on—they're all on the way up here."

Three days of menacing, sinister silence followed. The heat had built, day by day, minute by minute. Bones grew restless, irritated now, by the closed pigeon basket. The field mouse having gone elsewhere, Bones had only the pigeons with which to amuse himself. A linesman was passing along the trench with a reel of cable. Bones growled. Stanley looked at him anxiously. Bones hadn't growled for such a long time, but now he was as scrappy as a caged tiger. There was a swerve and a glitter to his eye today. Stanley glanced at the unused Field Message book, the green Army Book number 153 in which he was supposed to record his active duty, on the shelf next to the candle. Corporal Hunter liked to occupy Stanley with small jobs like the heliograph or the Aldis lamp.

Just beyond Fidget, the Devon Messenger was setting up his red and white flags and opening his black steel box. He came up each evening at rations time with the mail. Wherever he opened the box, that was the Battalion HQ Post Office. If the box was open and the flag up then the Post Office was in operation.

Stanley watched the Messenger, thinking how nice it would be to have more buns and honey. You only got parcels when you were back at base but he could write a card to Lara Bird now, to thank her and to ask how Da was. Then perhaps she'd send some more.

Stanley unearthed a postcard from his pack. It was rumpled and furry around the edges, only passable to send to your teacher if you were writing from a trench. Eleven days had gone by since he'd received her letter. Tom would know everything now. Stanley turned the postcard over and over in his hands. In England he'd wanted so much to get away that he'd never worried about Tom's reaction. Now he was in France he couldn't stop worrying about it. Would Tom force him home through the official channels? Was Tom still at home now or had his leave ended? Stanley put the postcard away. He wouldn't write a card to Lara Bird after all. He'd wait till he heard from Tom.

Stanley and Fidget walked past the Post Office and joined the line in the kitchen, heads bent.

It was very low, Cook's trench, you couldn't stand up in it. Two men in front were talking.

"Ludendorff's laying a new railway . . . his Railway Service is out, all hours, laying new sleepers for all the ammunition he's planning on bringing up." Fidget couldn't resist this kind of morose talk. "We're the last British battalion on the right—after us there's only the French . . ."

"Hello, kid, come and have some dinner . . ."

That's what Cook said to him every Rations-Up. Stanley had got used to the "kid" part of it, because Cook was friendly to him and kind to Bones. He, like most of the men, held Bones in a kind of slightly awed affection.

Back in his funk-hole, Stanley put down his mess tin with a grimace. What was the food like at the Front if it was this bad here? One loaf of gritty bread to twelve men and no hot rations was what Fidget said they got. Fidget was perching himself on an upturned crate, the sign that he was ready for rummy.

"The attack will come tomorrow," Fidget said for the umpteenth time, his tea-colored eyes jumping and starting. He seemed as certain of this as he had yesterday, and the day before, but now he was waving his arms and pointing in the direction of the piles of ammunition, high as houses, that were stacked all the way along the line.

They interrupted their game to watch as a couple of linesmen went over the top on their bellies with their pliers and their heavy reels of cable. It was a linesman's duty to lay and repair cables. No one liked doing it but the cables must be kept in good condition for the Fuller-phone. Along this front there were over seven thousand miles of buried, camouflaged cable. It was dangerous work. The land here wasn't good: if you dug more than three feet you reached water, and the enemy gunners made the linesmen and buried lines their special targets.

Stanley had an unbeatable hand—he stood to win five francs and was waiting for Fidget to play his card when Corporal Hunter approached with an Aldis lamp and rifle. It was difficult to move along the narrow trench with so much equipment and it was a good idea to keep out of the way whenever Hunter came by, so Stanley pulled Bones aside.

"Fidget, prepare the pigeons to go up. The radios aren't safe. They're too close, the Hun are picking up our signals. The pigeons will be collected in half an hour."

Hunter left.

"It'll come in the morning—the attack will come in the morning." An uneasy mix of pride and worry showed on Fidget's uncertain face. "He'll be relying on my pigeons."

There was no possibility of sleep that night. Cables and instruments were checked and double-checked, more lines laid. Linesmen and instrument repairers went in and out of the Signal Station. Stanley lay on his platform above Bones, listening to his breathing, wondering if Fidget was right this time.

4 April 1918

A few miles to the east of Villers-Bretonneux

At four thirty the following morning, the Allied lines stood to in darkness and in a worrying, wet fog. At four forty-five the enemy howitzers belched into fire, the enemy guns launching an onslaught that whisked the night into shooting tongues of flame. The earth itself was erupting, Stanley's heart pounding a tattoo to the thudding of the guns, the screaming of the howitzers tearing his eardrums, the veins in his temples throbbing.

Bullets howled and shrieked. Stanley kept a hand on Bones's head, but Bones, in this deep, dark trench, was calm, only slathering a little because to him the sound of shelling meant there must also be food.

A reluctant dawn broke and a murky light crawled across the battlefield. Out of the fog British airplanes appeared and disappeared again toward the enemy trenches. On and on, hour after unending hour, the fighting raged, all morning, every gun in the world firing, the whole plain alight with bursting shells, with savage crashes and fierce shrieks.

Deadened now to the noise, though still shaking with terror, Stanley watched and tried to decipher and disentangle the chaos that he saw. The shells that burst immediately on impact, throwing stones and dirt thirty yards up, were high explosives. Their splinters could fly two hundred yards and probably kill at that distance. The ones that burst in the air were shrapnel-type shells. The long guns gave a yelp when they fired, then a shriek, while the three-inch guns were a continuous crack and growl.

Hands trembling, Stanley took up the heavy trench periscope. Now he could see whatever was visible in such fog, without raising his head over the parapet. He wanted to check Corporal Hunter's forward observation posts.

Directly below Stanley's post was a British pill-box. That was the station in which Hunter's forward signalers were based and it was one of the three posts to which Hunter's buried cables were laid. Three communication lines, fifteen yards apart and parallel, laddered to each other every fifty yards, led from Hunter's Signal Station to each forward post. These lines could keep working with up to seventy breaks. Other lines led backwards from the Signal Station to the general Brigade HQ and the high-ranking officers.

Fidget slid around the wooden post of Stanley's dug-out, his brows shooting up and down his forehead. The noise was too loud to hear anything, but Fidget's skeletal hands were describing a pigeon rising, circling. Stanley was relieved to see that Fidget's fingers were shaking, that Fidget looked as terrified as himself. Fidget was gesturing now to the fog, now dipping his head and covering it with an arm. The pigeons wouldn't like the fog, he was saying, wouldn't fly in it. If I were Corporal Hunter, thought Stanley, I wouldn't set such store by a pigeon.

The Aldis lamp, though, would be even less use in fog,

and so would the heliograph. Fog presented the worst set of circumstances for a Signal Station. If the Corporal couldn't use radio, or pigeons, or the Aldis lamp, or the heliograph, he'd be depending on the cables holding and on runners, otherwise every battalion in the sector would be cut off from Brigade HQ.

"It's all right, Stanley," bellowed Fidget as he headed into the Signal Station. "They're holding the front line here. The Eighteenth are holding off the attack."

At midday the enemy fire intensified to a hurricane bombardment. Shells pounded the earth, throwing her guts to the skies, turning her inside out. Could communication lines still be working? How could they survive this shelling? The observation post (OP) below, the only one close enough to see in the thick fog, was being given a hammering. Stanley abandoned the periscope, the parapet shaking so that his field of vision jumped from one side of the plain to the other at each crash. How could anyone know what was happening?

Fidget returned, his changeable gooseberry eyes wide with alarm. "The Fourteenth Division—holding the front line to the north—they've fallen back."

Stanley took up his field glasses and, using his fingers, made his peephole bigger so that he could see out of both lenses. The OP was rocking like a boat before him. Suddenly it crumbled, dispersing into the air as though it had been built of flour.

A sapper cried out from the wooden stairs below, "No communication with the forward left Company about eight hundred yards on the east of the railway line."

Above the general roar, Fidget yelled into Stanley's ear, "It's cut the lines . . . The shelling's cut one of the lines."

On Corporal Hunter's orders, a pair of linesmen scuttled out over the top. Horrified, Stanley watched as they crawled, unprotected, down the slope with nothing but their reel of cable, their pliers, insulating tape, safety pins, and jackknives. You couldn't hope, surely, to keep telephone lines working when the whole world was being turned inside out. Would he be able to do that, Stanley wondered, if ordered to, to crawl down that desolate slope? The linesmen slithered on, running their hands along the lines, tapping and calling the Signal Station at intervals. Stanley heard, from down below, the Sappers' answers coming.

"A Company signals OK."

Then came another call from the Fuller-phone operator to Brigade HQ: "Cable repaired, line through to A Company."

"No communication with B Company," shouted the sapper. "No signal from B Company."

There was a sudden flickering like summer lightning. A thunder-shower of light and sparks and bluish shells burst on the far side of the canal.

From far ahead came the rattle of gongs and the pounding of empty brass cases with bayonets—that was the gas siren, the gas alarm. The Hun was answering British fire with gas shells.

"Get the men into the open!" someone in the Signal Station was screaming down the line. Sinister, thick green-yellow fumes billowed in the grey fog.

Stanley clutched Fidget's arm—out there, beneath them,

out there among the falling shells and spumes of earth, was a man, running toward their trench. Was that a runner from B Company? The runner grew closer, had almost reached the parapet. Corporal Hunter was there by the fire step, ready to let him in.

Stanley saw the runner speaking, heard the Corporal repeating his words, bellowing down the stairs, "Enemy outposts, enemy soldiers . . . behind the front line to the north-east . . . B Company forced back. One forward Signal Station destroyed. The Fourteenth have pulled right back. Enemy within four hundred yards of Villers."

Where was the other runner? They were always sent in pairs, even if they carried the same message, in the hope that one might get through. Stanley grabbed his field glasses, looked out and saw him—there—staggering up the open slope—a dark stain on his chest, a growing splodge of crimson creeping outward. How far had he run with that wound? His screams seemed to pierce the very earth, to lacerate the deafening roar of the guns. Stanley started forward on the fire step, but Corporal Hunter pulled him back and together they watched, helpless, as the runner collapsed, clutching his chest, stranded, dying only fifty yards from where they stood. Stanley was distraught, horrified. Could no one help? Fidget, and the men beyond—they'd all turned their heads away. Still Stanley watched that figure for any sign of life, watched till he saw red bubbles frothing at the mouth and nose. Then he, too, turned his head.

"They've pulled back, the front line's retreating!" shouted Hunter. "Forced back by the retreat of the Fourteenth."

Corporal Hunter took up Stanley's field glasses and raised

them to his eyes. Deep furrows were carved down his fore-head like twin valleys. Hunter shouted for two more lines-men over the top to repair the communication lines and as he did so, Stanley saw his eyes flicker over the parapet, to-ward the wall of flame along the far side of the canal. What chance of survival did the Corporal give the men? Did he know, even as they went out, that there was no chance of their coming back? Another linesman was fighting his way along the trench to Hunter.

"The shelling's cut the lines, sir . . . There's no point, sir, they're blown to bits as soon as they're laid."

"Oh God," breathed Hunter to the linesman, aghast and haggard. "No signals and we can't lay new lines till night-fall. We've only the runners and they haven't a chance—the Hun's taken the tunnel under the canal—they'd have to swim across."

Hunter raced back down to the Signal Station. There were more shouts from below, unintelligible. Fidget was shouting to Stanley that the front line had pulled back again, that it wasn't holding. A man came up the stairs, white-faced, eyes full of fear, a fresh runner, with Hunter behind. Hunter looked toward the canal and the sickle of flame that grew hourly closer.

Stanley looked at the face of the runner. And he looked down at Bones, willing and ready. Would he be wanted now? his round eyes seemed to ask. Stanley saw, with a rush of love, the large square skull and wing-like ears, and he felt a lump rising in his throat. Bones must go, a man should not be sent—the dog was faster, lower, had the better chance.

"No, sir. Don't send a man. S-send my dog, sir."

Hunter turned. "Send a dog?" He gave a mocking, irritated shake of his head.

"S-send the dog, sir," said Stanley. "Save the man and send the dog." Bones inched closer to Stanley, his tail flicking. "It's what he's trained for, sir."

Hunter looked over the plain.

"He's as good as a man, sir, better than a man. Send him up to B Company with the runner, sir, but let the dog run back with the message. He's a strong swimmer, sir."

"All right." Hunter closed his eyes and nodded. "All right," he said. "We'll give it a go."

The runner mouthed a heartfelt "God bless you" at Stanley.

The boy knelt on the duckboard floor in front of Bones. The dog was so tall, so proud, it made Stanley's heart ache.

"Do your best, Bones. It's important. Keep low. Come back. Above all, Bones, come back."

Stanley rose and handed the lead to the waiting runner.

Two hours later

A few miles to the east of Villers-Bretonneux

Both sides were waiting, both watching, both wary. The shelling had died down, the fog begun to burn away, the ravaged plain growing clearer. The front line was thin and sporadic, just platoons here and there. The observation posts of both A and B Company were just mounds of rubble. There was no communication line to C Company.

Hunter was at Stanley's side, listening to a linesman.

"Too many breaks, sir, there's too many breaks—we don't know where the men are—if the men are . . ."

Nauseous with worry, Stanley scoured the plain. Bones and the runner had been sent to B Company, or to where B Company had been, to the forward left, at Stanley's ten o'clock. To the north, this side of the Allied line, there were almost certainly, Fidget said, enemy outposts. Stanley had sent Bones up. He himself had sent the dog up. But it would be a hollow victory over the Fuller-phone if any harm came to Bones.

Hunter scanned the line along the canal for the hundredth time. Droplets of sweat coated his forehead. He turned abruptly to Stanley.

"Has he done it before? Has the dog worked in this sector before?"

"No, sir, but he'll do it. He can do it, sir."

The Corporal took his cap off to wipe his brow and Stanley realized, for the first time, that Hunter was not so much older than Tom.

"Has he ever worked in line before, anywhere in line?"

"No, sir, but he can do it, sir. He's as good as a man for the job."

Bones would do the work he knew so well, Stanley was certain of that. The dog would run home from anywhere, from any point of the compass. He was strong and he was fearless and if it were just a matter of running from the front line to the back line, Bones would do it—but if the front line was broken, if there were enemy outposts behind it . . .

"Has it come to this? To a dog?" asked Hunter, still wiping his brow.

Fidget grabbed Stanley, pointing. "Stanley—there!"

A shout went up from the kitchen, from Cook.

"The kid's dog—there—look!"

More shouts rippled along the trench.

"The boy's dog—his dog's at the canal!"

Two sappers rushed up and stood by Hunter. Stanley looked, his heart racing. There on the near side of the canal—there he was—the kingly giant—one hundred pounds of gleaming muscle—shaking himself—now loping away easily, unhurried. Now dropping into the sunken railway line. Stanley waited, breath held.

"Clever boy, clever boy, that's it, take cover," breathed Stanley. Minutes passed. Too long, too long—he should be up by now. Stanley glimpsed Hunter shaking his head from side to side. Stanley steadied himself. No, Hunter was wrong, the dog would come up, but where? Fidget clutched at Stanley again—pointing. The dog was out now, keeping tigerishly low to the ground, his brindled body unflinching, negotiating ridges and crests and jagged pieces of iron. They watched Bones make a semicircle around the high, firm edge of a crater.

"Astonishing . . ." said Hunter.

Stanley could see in his heart the black triangle ears and shining eyes, hear in his heart the firm tread of his paws. That little message around his neck, if only Bones knew it, would go from Hunter to Brigade HQ, then by dispatch rider to the Corps Commander and on by telephone to an Army HQ, from there to the HQ of the Commander-in-Chief and finally all the way across the Channel to the War Office.

Awash with pride, Stanley saw Bones racing across the ravaged plain. He himself had trained that dog, Stanley told himself, seeing himself opening the cylinder, pulling out the message, checking the time, noting it in his Army Record Book, handing the message to an amazed and grateful Hunter.

Stanley, Hunter, and Fidget all stood close, all intent on Bones. Beyond Fidget stretched a row of tense, watching men. Bones dropped into a shallow runnel and Stanley heard Hunter say, "Amazing . . . He's taking cover again . . ."

"Come, Bones, come," whispered Stanley.

There were perhaps only four hundred yards to go. Stanley

prepared to let the dog in, holding aside the trench netting over the fire step, fingering the titbit in his pocket, ready with the words, "Good boy, good."

A sudden mortar exploded to Bones's left and he was tossed skyward in a volcanic eruption of earth and flying steel. Frozen with horror, Stanley saw him, legs upward, like a stuffed toy. The ground fell away beneath Stanley. Numb and sick with dread he searched and searched again the area where he'd last seen the dog.

"Where did that come from?" said Hunter. "Can you see the dog?"

"There, sir, a hundred yards, sir, to the north, where the line's given way—there to the left—an enemy outpost behind the line!" shouted Fidget.

Hunter gripped Stanley's arm and pointed. "There—he's there—your dog's up . . ."

Stanley couldn't see at first, he was shaking so violently. Then he could—Bones was up, but facing the wrong way.

"Bones!" he shouted, starting on to the parapet. Hunter yanked him back. "Bones!" Stanley called again. Bones's head was turning one way, then the other. He was confused. The dog was flummoxed by his landing, or the shelling. Stanley rammed one fist into the other, sick with dread, but now Bones was racing away in a demented zigzag course perpendicular to that he'd started out on. On and on he went, his back end rounded and hunched. Hunter cursed. Stanley started up the fire step again. The dog was not well, he had to call him back—Bones never deviated from his course. "Bones!" he called. "Bones!"

Hunter pulled him back. "No . . . No . . ." Hunter's arm

was around his shoulder now. "Get down, stay low. Let the dog go."

Stanley shook himself free and started forward again.

"Get down, Ryder. That's an order," barked Hunter.

Two hours trickled by in quiet misery. Stanley combed the plain, inch by aching inch, again and again and again. If Bones were alive he'd come back; he'd been hit perhaps, but he'd been able to run.

The tangle of wire and weeds on the parapet grew dark and indistinct. In the far distance to the north, the enemy guns began again their grumbling and their winking stabs and flashes of light. Knowing that Stanley was waiting for Bones, wouldn't leave his dug-out till the dog came in, Corporal Hunter carried Stanley's rations to him. Hunter said nothing but Stanley felt his despair, the despair of all the Devons, whose hope lay in the cylinder around Bones's neck. Hunter placed Stanley's rations on the platform, rested a hand on Stanley's shoulder and said, "Eat, Ryder, you must—" He stopped, open-mouthed, ghastly pale, looking along the length of the trench. "Ryder . . ." Hunter's voice died away.

At the end of straight bay, the section of trench beyond Fidget, stood Cook, a candle in his hand. Now men were rising, some still holding their mess tins, rising in a wave and standing aside, in silent horror.

"Ryder—your dog—he's made it back . . ." Again Hunter's whispered words tailed away.

Stanley leaped forward, then stopped. Bones was stumbling, unsure of his legs, of his ground, of his direction—what was wrong? He was staggering, legs buckling, and head low, grazing the ground—what was wrong? Those eyes—they were gooey, oozing. Bones couldn't see. Terrible to watch, blind and staggering, all grace gone, every bending step the heartbreaking depiction of nobility, courage, and loyalty.

Cook's candle was passed down the line. More candles were lit by the men who stood aside, a fitting guard of honor for the great dog stumbling on between them, hocks and stifles bent double.

Not wanting to confuse Bones, Stanley took a slow, deliberate step, holding out his hand, now moving closer again. Bones's ears flickered. He raised his head an inch or two.

"Good boy, good," Stanley whispered. Bones took another buckling step. One more and he reached his master, staggering, falling at Stanley's feet. A second passed. "Good boy, good," Stanley was whispering, but now, with the last of his strength, Bones was straining to rise, to straighten his trembling forelegs, to lift his head to his master.

Stanley saw his ears prick, his tail quiver, and he saw the gummed-up, damaged eyes.

"Good boy, good." With fumbling, useless fingers, Stanley unclasped the cylinder and took out the message, then handed it to Hunter.

Bones's head thudded to the ground, his jowls loose and sprawling on the dusty duckboards.

Fidget was wringing his hands. "Gas, Stanley, he's been gassed. Shoot him . . . kindest thing . . . to shoot him."

"I'll shoot you before I shoot this dog." Stanley heard the anger in Hunter's voice, turned and saw him wipe his eyes as he tried to read the message.

There was a new note of panic as Hunter, still reading, shouted for a sapper.

"B Company are holding Boche prisoners. There's no front line to speak of there—they're trapped—surrounded on three sides, two hundred feet to the right of the intersection of the road and the sunken railway line. All signaling equipment destroyed before leaving the post. The prisoners have revealed a further attack coming tonight. Twenty-hours." Hunter looked up. "That's minutes—fifteen minutes from now—we've no front line in this sector—we're sitting ducks." Hunter handed the message to the sapper, whirled around to Stanley, then away again, hesitated, and turned back.

"Fifteen minutes . . . Good God! . . . Thank God, Ryder, for your dog. I'd never have believed it if I hadn't seen it with my own eyes." Hunter leaped away, shouting for an AVC man, for a veterinary man, as he ran down to the Signal Station.

Minutes later, there was panic and disorder all along the line.

"Move backwards. Move backwards. Take up position in the support lines."

"Back down the trench. Get back, back down the trench."

"Keep moving backwards."

Amid the flood of men heading for the communication trench, Stanley sat alone, cradling Bones's head, searching Bones's flank for wounds with panicked, jittery fingers. Only fifteen minutes till the Hun attack. He felt a sharp prick in the pad of a finger. Along the lower edge of exposed flank, along the line of the belly, ran a deep gash, the length of a child's arm, the skin ripped, the pink and white guts laced with barbs of steel. Stanley made a choking sound, hands trembling helplessly above the ragged skin. Blind. Wire in his guts and with gas in his lungs. Oh, when would someone come to help them? He couldn't carry the dog—would they be left behind as everyone retreated?

All around there were confused shouts and yells. A stream of men poured along the communication trench, the remnants of a whole division surging past in headlong retreat. Stanley leaped up and spun around. A stretcher—he must find a stretcher. Senselessly he looked over the parapet. Trailing shadows morphed into men, tattered and ghoulish figures that stumbled toward the communication trench in heavy boots and huge helmets, rifles for crutches. Where the trench was too congested, men clambered into the open, scrambling over crumbling ridges and pits, past broken carts and wagons. A heavy-gun team plowed uphill, the terrified gunners whipping and cursing their mounts onward. One infantryman was pushing another, purple-faced, with red-rimmed bulging eyes, in a wheelbarrow. A wheelbarrow! Stanley could move Bones in a barrow—where—where could he find another barrow?

"Stanley. Quick."

It was Fidget. Fidget with a stretcher. Stanley was overwhelmed with relief and gratitude.

"Quick, Stanley. Get him on. Quick." Fidget was strapping his pigeon basket to his back.

Beyond the parapet someone shouted, "Where's the front line?"

"There isn't one."

Stanley unraveled the stretcher on the platform and together they lifted the helpless dog on, while all around them, men shouted and cursed. "Keep moving backwards. Hurry. Out of the way. Into the reserve lines. Move on. Move on."

Stanley and Fidget forced their way into the rush of men flooding back to the support lines, reached the intersection with the communication trench, and—within seconds of turning—heard a confusion of bursting shells and crashing walls.

There were alarmed yells and screams from scattered men running toward the back line.

"It's in enemy hands—the front line—all in enemy hands!"

"The Hun's got posts and bits of trench a hundred and fifty yards away!"

"The enemy's following behind—"

Another savage crash made Stanley leap out of his skin as dirt and earth rained into the communication trench.

"Oh God," said Fidget as he and Stanley turned to each other in horror, blinking away dust and debris, wiping sweat and grime from their faces. Both glanced backward with the same fear.

"Here, take this." Stanley thrust his end of the stretcher into the nearest hands and leaped up. The roof of the Signal Station had fallen in. Smoke was pouring out. Hunter would have been in there destroying equipment before abandoning it. Stanley saw a tall figure reach the fire step, stagger two paces and fall, writhing. "Hunter," he breathed.

Hunter's body gave a sudden, short spasm, then went rigid. There was another explosion. Insensible with shock, Stanley dropped back into the communication trench, looked at Fidget and moved his head slowly from side to side. "Hunter," he said. "They got Hunter."

The Devon man holding the stretcher shoved it back into Stanley's hands.

In the support line an officer was holding up a rifle to stop runaways, bellowing, "Halt! Stand firm. Take that section!"

He let Stanley and Fidget pass, waving them in the direction of a Veterinary First Aid Station. They weaved their way past labor units digging fresh graves, past a line of the walking wounded wrapped in blankets at a Regimental Aid Post, between stretcher-bearers, carts, ammunition stores, and columns of fresh men, all the while Stanley whispering over and over to Bones, "Bones, stay with me, Bones, stay. Hang on. You'll be all right, you'll be all right . . ."

"There." Fidget pointed to a horse-drawn cattle float, by the side of which a pair of men were treating a wounded dog on a small wooden table. An AVC officer with a thin, hunted face approached and cast a weary eye over Bones.

"Gas . . . bad case."

Mutely Stanley guided the man's fingers to the barbed wire in Bones's belly. The officer looked up and said, "It's not a case for the Mobile Units."

Dizzy with the compounded terror and horror of the day, Stanley covered his eyes as he spoke.

"Is there n-no hope?"

The vet took his hand. "We treat hundreds of animals every day, and seventy percent or so are not fit enough to return to the front line."

"What h-happens to—to those not fit enough to return?"

There was heartache in the officer's voice as he answered.

"We've orders to shoot animals that can't be released fit for active service."

With a gentle squeeze he released Stanley's hand and directed him to a motorized horse ambulance and Veterinary Hospital number 10. Fidget helped load Bones into the truck and turned to leave.

"Good luck, Stanley," he said. "God bless your dog."

Alone in the ambulance, Stanley wept openly for Bones, who'd run blindfold through a battle so many worlds beyond his comprehension.

The night of 4 April 1918

Veterinary Hospital number 10, Neufchâtel, near Etaples

Together, Bones and Stanley traveled alone a short distance through the night, the driver picking his way without headlights along a glimmering, potholed road, passing infantry, cavalry, and endless ammunition limbers until they arrived at what looked like a big white circus tent. A white flag with a blue cross flapped from a mast.

Orderlies collected Bones from the ambulance and carried him past dimly lit mess buildings, dipping vats, isolation huts with latticed windows, pneumonia wards, and mange wards, to an operating theater.

An officer wearing a white apron over his khaki, his eyes circled with dark creases, approached.

"Lieutenant Fielding, Jolyon Fielding." He stuck out his hand. Behind Fielding stood rows of horses, in splints or bandaged, being cleaned and dressed.

Fielding put a hand on Bones's heart, studying Stanley as he did so. He pulled the blanket down. In the yellow lantern light they both saw the striped coat gleaming like candlelit velvet, and below, the pink and white guts, the metal barbs.

"Oh . . ." Fielding looked up. "Did he—did he run home like this?"

Stanley nodded, voiceless. Fielding held his gaze for a second or two, then shook his head.

"There's nothing I can do. I'm sorry." Fielding took Stanley's hand. "He's very little time left. You must stay with him to the end."

Still mute, Stanley nodded again. Fielding watched as Stanley climbed up on to the table and lay beside the dog.

"Good boy, good," said Stanley, and he laid his head next to Bones, his hand on the dog's flank, feeling its faint rising, faint falling. Fielding pulled the blanket over them and said he'd be back before long.

"Good boy . . . good. Go, go, boy, let go," whispered Stanley, caressing the tall ears, the deep muzzle. "Let go." Silent tears coursed down his cheeks. "Go, boy, go."

An hour or so passed before Stanley felt the quiver of a single ear against his own cheek, gentle as the beat of a wing.

The next morning

Etaples

Drunk with exhaustion, disembodied with grief, Stanley walked unseeing, unhearing, past tents, past troops, toward Central Kennel HQ, no soft padding at his heels, no large head to rest a hand on. He had one single idea in his head: to go home, to go to Lara Bird, to Nethercott. He'd collect his pay, tell them he was underage, and he'd leave.

"Keeper Ryder, sir." Stanley saluted the Major at the desk of Central Kennel HQ.

"Ah." The officer leaped to his feet. "Keeper Ryder." He moved around his desk to stand in front of Stanley. "I'm sorry, lad. Corporal Hunter cabled to say . . . We heard, Ryder, we all heard what your dog did."

"Corporal Hunter?" Stanley asked dully.

The Major nodded, closing his eyes. "Yes, he cabled to say the battalion was saved, by the message your dog carried. Not C Company. There—there was nothing anyone could do—but the back lines, the remains of the front line, they got back. Ten minutes after Hunter sent his last cable, the Station was hit. He was killed outright. That cable said the dog deserves a VC, that his courage and sense of duty were the equal of any man."

Numb and helpless, Stanley allowed himself to be steered by the Major toward the door.

"They counterattacked in the late afternoon with fresh troops—the Australians under Colonel Milne took two German divisions. Well, we haven't stopped the Hun dreaming of Villers yet, but we've kept him off for a bit."

Stanley, lagging a little behind the Major, kicked at the white dust.

"You're one of our best men, Ryder. We'll get you back up there as soon as we can."

"No . . . no. I don't, I don't—I *won't*—go back up, I don't want another dog."

"Follow me." The Major seemed to be practiced at not hearing. "We've a dog waiting. The vet will tell you about him. Something else might turn up, but start on this one, and we'll soon get you back to the Front."

With no strength to resist, Stanley found himself being led to the Kennels' Veterinary Hut where he was passed, like a helpless child, from the Major who wished him well, to Lieutenant-Colonel Thorne. Thorne was steering Stanley around to the back of the hut. He took lots of little, fast steps on small, rather dainty feet. Thorne was all chest, his hips and legs tailing away like a tadpole's.

"Here he is. Pistol."

Stanley didn't look at the dog, was looking directly at Thorne; he didn't want to be given another dog. Thorne was all puffed-up and pigeon-chested. His face was bird-like, too, round-eyed and sharp-nosed, but he was smiling now, his face crinkling into a bright, surprisingly likeable smile, and he seemed to want some kind of response from Stanley.

Stanley looked and saw, briefly, a still, silent dog, coiled on the dusty ground, some sixty feet or so away. Stanley looked back at the Lieutenant-Colonel.

"I don't want a new dog. I want to go home."

The Lieutenant-Colonel had probably heard this before, Stanley realized—was as practiced as the Major at shepherding men back into line—but Stanley had nothing to give, no strength, no love, no courage; he had been emptied by grief and loss. He wanted, simply, to be at home. Soldier and Bones had taken all of him with them. He looked away over the blinding white expanse, through the rows of kennels to the tents beyond. He saw only a world drained of color and feeling. So many men, so many men, but still a boy could drown in his own aloneness. Yet, if Bones had not run home, Stanley thought dully, he too would have been in that Signal Station, he too would have died.

"You could do the dog some good, help him along . . . He's had a bad shock."

Thorne was drawing tentatively closer to the dog. It rose to its feet and whipped around, snarling, cringing, curling its lips, baring its teeth. It was hairless in places, with tufts of hair the color of steel in others. Its listless eyes made Stanley want to look away, feared to see the head that hung like a weight, the flesh dotted with open sores. The dog widdled where it stood without so much as lifting a leg. Now it was crouching and cowering, every fiber expressing extreme fear. The Lieutenant-Colonel, looking a little hurt, had scuttled back to stand by Stanley.

"What happened?" asked Stanley simply. "Who did

this?" The dog crouched so low that the raw skin of its belly grazed the ground.

"Well. It's a long story . . . This urchin was a stray, rounded up by police in Liverpool. They're not killing strays any more, you see, that's how Colonel Richardson got him. Macy, the vet, treated him—he'd a bad case of sarcoptic mange, that's why the skin's rough, like a hide in places. Macy gave him a mange wash and its been on the mend for a while now."

Stanley was looking away, far beyond the tents. I could just start walking, he was thinking, just turn around and walk and walk till I get to the boats.

"Now look, Keeper Ryder, this dog might not look much but he's muscular and light, he's strong and he's clever. They have brains usually, these summer breeds, and it's cleverness that you want. He's good—you won't have to teach him any-thing."

The dog whimpered and dribbled more urine, feather-less tail tucked low between its legs, and then sank down to the ground it had just puddled.

"No," Stanley would have shouted to the skies if there'd been any strength in him, but he simply looked at Lieutenant-Colonel Thorne and shook his head. "No," he repeated out loud. He would be heard. He *would* go home.

Perhaps all officers were used to men saying no, because the Lieutenant-Colonel was still speaking. "Don't be put off by his looks. You see there, around his neck—those patches of skin were very sore, but now they're softer—see?—bristling with new hair. He'll look better every day. Earn his trust and you'll make him a good soldier."

Stanley saw the dry cracked skin around the ears, the patches of raw flesh. He felt spiritless, sickened, then turned away, unable to fight his revulsion. It wasn't lovable, this dog, it wasn't like Bones. No dog could ever be like Bones. Thorne was stepping inside his hut, perhaps to fetch something.

"N-n-n-no," said Stanley, too late for Thorne to hear him. "I won't go back up."

Remote, and disconnected from all around him, Stanley was still thinking, I will just walk, walk and walk and if they stop me, I'll tell them I'm too young.

The grey dog gave a strange, heart-rending whimper, prodding Stanley from his dreams. In spite of himself, in spite of his weariness, Stanley crouched and remained a minute or so looking at the dog.

"Why are you so sad?" he whispered.

Still crouching, Stanley moved forward. The dog flinched and whipped back with a shotgun reflex, baring his teeth.

"You're all spent, aren't you? As empty and all gone as I am." Numb with exhaustion, revulsion, and pity, the boy stayed there, head bowed now over his arms. Thorne was at the door, holding out a collar, message cylinder, and lead. "Wh-what happened? What happened to him?" Stanley burst out. "M-mange, mange on its own—mange doesn't do this to a dog."

The Lieutenant-Colonel took a deep breath, his chest inflating beyond all reasonable probability.

"Pistol saw a short spell of active service but his keeper . . . well, his keeper got shell shock—a bad case, nasty case. He lost his head and lashed out, picked up a gun"—Thorne covered his eyes—"so we were told—held it to the dog's head and fired . . ."

Stanley reeled. Pistol's own master had picked up a gun . . . Thorne was still talking.

"Someone stepped in and pushed the barrel aside, but the dog knew . . ."

To point a gun, Stanley was thinking, at a dog that would give his all, his everything, for you! Disgusted and sickened, Stanley looked at the innocent grey dog on the ground.

"Oh," he said. "Oh . . ."

A few minutes passed.

Stanley moved a little closer.

"No wonder," he whispered. "No wonder." Still crouching, keeping his hands by his sides, Stanley moved forward again.

The dog turned his head toward the boy. A second or so passed and the dog's nose twitched, then twitched again. He blinked and slunk forward two or three paces, stifles bent almost to the ground, then stopped and waited, nose twitching. He began to quiver. His brows flickered up and down, his hairless tail flipped across the sand, raising clouds of dust. Stanley stayed where he was. The dog was quivering now from head to tail. Thorne was silent, watching. The dog slunk closer and his tail flipped once more. Slowly Stanley opened his palm flat beneath the long narrow jaws. Slower still, he inched it up to the sore, cracked skin under the neck and further up around the ears. The dog rested his long snout on the boy's lap, his tail whipping back and forth.

"Well, I never," said Thorne, looking pleased, his chest swelling.

"Everyone else," whispered Stanley, "everyone else is sad too. Broken. Terrified. Every man here." Stanley kept whispering, now edging his hand back along the dog's flank, feeling the seismic shivering beneath his fingers. "I can see the whites of your eyes. You're terrified too, aren't you? You don't know or care, do you? You're beyond caring . . ."

Pistol was a mix of some kind; it would be difficult to tell what he was until his coat improved, but he was broad-chested and leggy—all long nose, slender limbs, and no belly. Stanley saw the dog's seriousness, his soulfulness, and felt, like a knife wound, Bones's humor, his truculence, his naivety, his bullish enthusiasm. Stanley bowed his head. No, he thought, I have no strength myself, I am myself too weak to look after you. I cannot look after myself. Stanley moved his hands so they were beneath the dog's jaws and lifted its head from his lap, feeling as he did so the dry scabs behind the ears.

"No." Stanley half rose, saying to himself, "I can't go back up, can't take another dog." To Thorne he said, "No. I can't. I can't do this."

Thorne looked upset, then distraught as the dog reared up and clung pitifully to Stanley's legs.

"No," said Stanley to Pistol. "Stay. Sit." To Thorne he said, "No. I'm going home."

Stanley turned on his heels before he could hear Thorne's response and marched away. He'd go back to the Major and tell him he was underage, that he wanted to go home. At the door to HQ, Stanley paused, seeing with a wave of irritation that the strange, silent dog was suddenly at his side.

"No. Go. Go." The dog looked grief-stricken. Stanley's exasperation grew. "No. Get away. Go."

The dog stood his ground, full of conviction that it was in the right place.

"Go. Boy. Go."

It lifted a forepaw. Where did the boy want him to go, if not here?

"Go, boy, go."

Stanley stood between the door and the dog, frustrated. He must speak to the Kennel Staff, must say straight away that he was going home—but he must also rid himself of the dog. He turned and marched back to Thorne's hut. The dog trotted light as a wisp alongside him, long snout raised to the boy's hand. Stanley marched faster, angry with himself, angry at this wretched grey dog. The dog followed right at his heels, head upward, jaws open in a half-smile.

"No," Stanley hissed at last. "I don't want you. I'm going home."

The strange grey dog nuzzled Stanley's legs. Stanley shook him off and marched on.

Thorne was waiting by the door. He'd seen everything. Stanley took Bones's lead out of his pocket, attached it firmly to Pistol, and handed it to Thorne.

"No. I will not go. It is no place for a dog."

Thorne's small head was nodding up and down, compassionate and patient, as though coaxing a recalcitrant, wounded animal, but Stanley didn't want compassion or understanding, he wouldn't give Thorne time to speak, and his quick cross steps blew up clouds of dust as he marched away.

He reached the blue and white crossed flags of Central Kennels HQ and turned to check, before entering, that Thorne still had the dog. As he did so, he saw the dog tear around and rip the leash through Thorne's fingers, watching horrified as the dog flew toward him, racing with every fiber in his body, back coiled, tail outstretched, neck outstretched, his smooth, liquid movement, his entire form, the perfect expression of a powerful, single-minded will. Thorne's head was bobbing sadly against his chest and Stanley found himself liking the man for being more affected by the dog's distress than by his own insubordinate behavior. It arrived at Stanley's feet and sat, his eyes narrowed, panting, his tail whirring, grinning up at the boy.

"Stanley, laddie, is it you?" The boy turned from the maddening, grinning dog to the familiar voice. It was Hamish, the same Hamish who'd always looked out for him at Chatham, running toward him.

Hamish hugged Stanley, then with a hand on each shoulder, drew back and looked at him carefully. "Aye, they told me"—he tipped his head toward the HQ—"they told me about your dog."

A sudden wave of grief washed over Stanley and he nodded dumbly.

"They say he was a great dog . . ."

When Stanley came to, Hamish was bending down, caressing the strange, silent grey dog. Stanley shook his head.

"I'll never have another dog, Hamish, never."

"Aye, this fellow's no' so bad . . . there's deerhound in it somewhere . . . Aye, he'll be canny enough . . . a good 'un. Silent too"—Hamish tousled Pistol's raw ears—"like his master." Hamish grinned at Stanley, then turned back to the dog. "Poor wee thing, your heart's in the Highlands, so it is. You're mebbe still young?" Hamish pushed back the slender lips. "Ever so young. Same age perhaps as a nine-year-old child. Aye, with a summer breed a puppy can surprise you as it grows. You'll be thinking it's going to be medium-sized and smooth and—look—it's a shaggy giant." Hamish grinned and tousled the dog's ears again. "Aye, 'tis a Highland hound, sure enough, the sum and substance of the canine species no less, laddie." To the dog he said then, "Aye, you're a cracker, you are."

Hamish looked at Stanley once more, scrutinizing him.

"Come, ah've got two signaler's bikes and we'll go and get something to eat . . . That's the fun about these blue and white bands, we've more freedom to move around than the poor old infantry, and you look like you've no' eaten in a wee while. Will we take this fellow along too?"

Stanley paused and half turned, saw Thorne nodding again, happily now. He'd wanted to go home, but to what? Where was Tom? If he returned home, he would miss the letter from Tom, which was surely on its way. Hamish put an arm around him and once again Stanley allowed himself to be led.

The army bicycle was much heavier than Stanley's old bicycle at Thornley and cycling on cobbles was bumpy. Biting back his tears, and focusing on the road as he went, Stanley told Hamish about Bones in an unstoppable flood of words. They passed a sign offering one egg and fried potatoes and tea and butter and pastries, all for 2 francs 40.

"Aye, and that's more words together in one go than I've heard before," said Hamish, studying Stanley as he pulled up at a second sign, offering two eggs and fried potatoes and tea and butter and pastries, again all for 2 francs 40. "This is the business," said Hamish, resting his bicycle against the sign. "Keep talking, laddie."

Stanley ate ravenously, surprised by his hunger, unable to remember when he'd last eaten. He felt better for being with Hamish, better for the eggs and fried potatoes and the warm crusty bread and the milk that wasn't powdered, but his hand kept slipping to his side, and in place of the large square skull of Bones there was this leggy animal, light as a whisper or a shadow, and always at his side.

10 April 1918

Etaples

Stanley and Pistol were making their way toward the dunes. Yesterday Hamish had told Stanley that his brother, James, had orders to go up to the Front, that he too was going up, would be serving under James. Two brothers working together. Stanley, after so many months away from home, had still not found Tom. There'd still been no letter. Nothing from Father Bill either, from the priest with the shiny spurs. Nothing from anyone. Surely he'd hear any minute now from Tom. As soon as Lara Bird had told Tom, then surely he'd have written.

Stanley felt a wet nose in his hand. The dog was nuzzling him. The dog's strange and immediate affection for Stanley felt at times like a burden too heavy, too great for so empty a heart, but he said with forced jollity, "Obstacle course. Obstacle course again for you today." Pistol's brows flickered and his tail circled. In spite of himself, Stanley smiled as he handed the dog over to a kennel orderly to lead away.

Each day those tufts of new hair had grown thicker, were deepening to slate grey, but the coat was all wrong, so long and rough and unfamiliar after the trim velvet pile of Bones.

That and Pistol's slightness. Where Stanley would always expect a solid, muscular weight against his legs, there instead would be this quicksilver shadow, all limb and nose.

The signal was given and the dogs were unleashed by the orderlies. Pistol was off, soaring over the first jump, over the second, then the third and highest, a five-bar gate, with grace and joy and ease, hind legs tucked. The dog could jump like a stag, Stanley had to admit to himself; he'd never seen a dog jump like that.

They were all racing home now, hurtling down through the pinewoods, flinging themselves on to the sand and over the dunes. There was Pistol. Stanley caught his breath: the dog had a way of surprising him—that gallop was so very fast, so fast you could barely tell, now, he was a dog, his hind legs thrusting springs that reached his chin at each take-off. He was at the front, a flurry of dogs in his wake, open-jawed, legs coalescing in an eternally suspended step. He smiled as he ran, his long jaws open, silvery tail aft like a banner, those soft breech feathers flying, back arched, the endless forelegs outstretched.

"He's a new dog, Keeper Ryder." Lieutenant-Colonel Thorne had joined Stanley. "Took to you from the start. He's had a rough time, though. Be gentle with him." Thorne paused a little before saying, "Remember that all he does, he does for you."

Stanley made a sort of involuntary, snorting sound. The responsibility for this dog was too much for so numb and glazed a heart as his own, but he recovered himself and looked up and said simply, "Yes, sir."

When Pistol arrived, eyes narrowed, panting and breathless and grinning, Stanley was caught up, just a little, in the dog's silvery joy.

Later, holding a tin of apricots and some chocolate, Stanley went once again to the Post Office, just in case there was a letter. As he approached, the postal orderly raised an arm, beckoning. He looked pleased to be able to give Stanley good news, after so many days of saying a cheerful "Sorry, nothing today."

Stanley's heart was in his mouth as he took the envelope, an official one, a letter telegram, stamped "URGENT BEF. ON ACTIVE SERVICE" across the top left with an officer's stamp dated 9 April. Tom! It must be from Tom. Why had he sent a letter telegram? He'd know that the Censor would read every word. There were lots of British stamps fixed to the telegram itself, 2d for every word—lots of stamps and, for a telegram, lots of words. Stanley ripped it open.

> Home on leave. Da's disappeared. Lara says not in his right mind when last seen. He left note, "I WAS NOT FAIR ON THE BOY. I DID HIM WRONG BUT THE DOG CAN'T BE GOT BACK." You must return—whatever has happened, there is more at stake here than a puppy. COME HOME.
> Tom.

Tom didn't ask how his little brother was, what work he was doing, if he was safe. It was so unlike the Tom he loved; so angry—that was it—so *angry*. Tom didn't want to see Stanley, just wanted him back because Da had disappeared. And that seemed to be all Stanley's fault. "There is more at stake here than a puppy." Tom meant that something might happen to Da. Tom was more concerned for Da than for his brother.

Shocked, Stanley leaned for support against a stack of crates of provisions. Could Tom not see that Stanley had signed up because he needed to be with Tom? "No," he said aloud, furious and wounded. "No. I am not going home." He screwed the telegram into an angry ball. He couldn't count on Tom any more than he could on Da.

Stanley marched furiously toward his tent. Too much, too much, it was too much to bear. It wasn't his fault that Da had disappeared. He marched faster, swinging his arms, wishing he could breathe a dragon's fire, to warn men, to warn the world, to warn Tom off him.

He reached his tent, heard chatter and laughter, and stopped. He couldn't go in. Couldn't go where men talked and laughed and read their brothers', sisters', mothers' letters to each other. He turned, gazing blankly at the immense, lonesome sea of tents. Lost and purposeless he stood, still holding the scrunched telegram, the apricots, and the chocolate. There was nowhere to be alone in a camp of ten thousand men.

Stanley drifted aimlessly along the paths he knew until he found himself at Central Kennels and he went, unthinking, to his dog's kennel. He'd not have to talk to the dog.

He could be silent and yet not be alone. If Tom didn't want his brother, if Da didn't want his son, the dog could have him. Stanley could belong to the strange grey dog.

Pistol was there waiting for Stanley as though he'd expected him all along, as though he'd wait all night, if necessary. Without greeting him, Stanley slumped against the kennel and just sat, with the apricots on his lap and the telegram in his hand. Bones would have been interested in the chocolate, but Pistol wasn't.

"Strange thing you are," he said, aware how intently Pistol was watching his face, his every movement. "More interested in me than in chocolate, eh?" he said amused. If he kept still, Stanley was thinking, the dog kept still; if he moved, the dog moved. Stanley tested him. If he looked to the right, would Pistol look to the right? Yes. If he looked to the left, would Pistol look to the left? Yes.

"You'd be better off thinking about chocolate than me," he said sadly.

Stanley covered his face with his hands, wishing his heart were not so numb.

The tin of apricots rolled off his lap. Stanley's hand was in his pocket, gripping the matchbox he'd carried since leaving home, the one which held the reed whistle. Da had never picked up the whistle Stanley had made for him—nothing meant anything to Da any more, not now that all the love had gone out of him and the anger had come into him.

The matchbox was rhomboid now after being squished by the Mills bombs, the words "Bryant & May" scarcely legible. Stanley forced it open, saw the reed whistle, saw in it the thorn trees and valleys and stone walls of home.

Miserable, Stanley put the whistle to his lips and blew, feeling the vibration of the reed. The call his da had taught him bubbled, bright and clear in the dusty air. Stanley's longing for home ballooned. Pistol leaped up at the whistle, frantic, nuzzling Stanley. Still lost in thoughts of Thornley, Stanley shook him off, irritated.

"Down, boy . . . Down. Inside. Kennel."

Leaving the apricots and the chocolate on the ground, Stanley rose. Holding the reed and the telegram, he walked away, glancing back only to ensure the dog didn't follow. Seeing the crestfallen ears, the light, graceful legs and hesitant tail, Stanley turned back and stroked the rough skin where the mange had been.

"It's you and me, just you and me." The dog opened its slender jaws and did his odd smiling thing. Stanley glimpsed the sharpness of Pistol's teeth, was stopped short by the puppyish whiteness of them.

"Hamish was right. You're younger than they think. You know, they don't like to take dogs under a year. Well, I'm too young too, but I'm staying. I can do this job as well as any man, and so can you."

14 April 1918

Etaples

It had been a good start to the day. Stanley had gone around twice for breakfast, kept his head down, and got a second lot. Even though Hamish had gone, still it had been good because instead of Church Parade there was Bathing Parade, a four-mile march over clumps of spiky grass, past hazy fishing boats, toward a classy seaside resort.

Stanley stripped. How good it would be to wash off the white dust. Already the other men were in the water, laughing and splashing and swimming with their dogs. The salt water would be good for Pistol—salt water was always good for skin problems, Da used to say. Stanley raced into the waves, threw himself in head first, enjoying the shock of cold, clean water. He rose and shook his head and turned to the shore, looking over the ramshackle pink and grey roofs of the town, toward the white tents of the camp that crawled up the hill like white sails, beyond them to the pine trees and hills.

Pistol was there on the shore running back and forth, thrilled, prancing at the waves, retreating as they broke, hectic with anxiety to reach Stanley, filled with trepidation about the waves. Bones, thought Stanley, would have been indignant at the waves. Like Canute, he'd expect the sea to retreat before him. Stanley smiled a sad smile.

Pistol thrust his head into Stanley's hand, clung as close as a shadow, when Stanley ran up and down the beach. This dog clung so tightly to Stanley that other keepers noticed and were jealous. Always in Pistol's eyes was the question, What do you want me to do?

Breathless, Stanley threw himself on to the shell-white sand and flung back his head to bask in the sun. Pistol settled beside him. Later, when Stanley sat up, Pistol sat too, and followed his master's gaze out to sea. Over that shimmering blue sea, the boy was thinking, lay England and Da and Tom.

Irritated by the direction of his thoughts, Stanley shook himself and leaped up. "Chocolate," he said to Pistol. "I've got five francs. When we get back, we'll have chocolate and apricots again in the YMCA."

Hamish had gone up to the Villers sector with his brother James, who was now a Captain in command of a Signal Station of ten men. Stanley had heard that another attack was expected in the sector. The news from there had grown worse, Amiens still the focus of Ludendorff's attention. Some ground had been lost, some gained, since Stanley had come out of the line; just inches, both ways.

At camp that evening a letter was waiting for Stanley, Tom's handwriting on the envelope.

"What now, Pistol? What will Tom say now?" said Stanley in a resigned voice, and began to read aloud for the benefit of the attentive dog.

Thornley
12 April 1918
Dear Brother,
My leave is to be cut short. I am under orders to return two days from now. It has been a difficult time here. Lara's father was killed on active service a month ago, Da is still missing. There has been much grief and much anxiety for you and for Da, but also great happiness. Lara and I were married yesterday at St Mary's. It wasn't right, you and Da not being there, but with the world so uncertain and my being forced to return early, we felt it best to press on.

Da still not at home? Why? Surely he'd have wanted to be there when Tom was on leave? "I am under orders to return two days from now": Tom was coming back—would be back in France soon.

Lara and I have talked so much of you
and of what drove you away and I now
know that you have suffered so much
more than I'd realized. I blame myself
for leaving you alone with Da when, deep
down, I knew he wasn't himself. I won't
force you home, but I _will_ search for you
to the four corners of France and I _will_
beg you to return. Lara will look after
you at Nethercott and things will be so
very different. Please know that my last
telegram was written more in fear for
you, in fear for Da, than in the anger
which I showed. I was so frightened for
you that I didn't know which way to
turn. Da can look after himself and you
— you must not concern yourself for
him, must only stay safe.

Stanley smiled and drew Pistol close. Tom was once again
himself.

I cannot bear that anything should
happen to you, cannot bear to think that
you are seeing the things I've seen. I
pray that Colonel Richardson is right,
that your work keeps you behind the
lines. And in spite of everything I long
to hear of it as I've seen many dogs
working for the enemy but no dogs of our
own.

I will write as soon as I arrive in
France. Stay safe, Stanley, till I find
you.

Your loving Tom.

Tom was on his way to France!

Stanley stuffed the letter into his pocket and hurried to
Central Kennels, the last to join the ranks of men assembled to listen to General Haig on the wireless, the words of
Tom's letter still running like a current in his head as the
General's voice boomed out.

"Three weeks ago today, the enemy began his terrific attacks against us . . ."

Tom didn't blame Stanley for Da's disappearance, but
somehow Stanley was beginning to feel that it was perhaps

his fault. The specter of the old man, white-haired, snatching at the empty air, had returned to trouble and unsettle him.

"His object is to . . . destroy the British Army . . . Every position must be held to the last man: there must be no retirement. With our backs to the wall, and believing in the justice of our cause, each one of us must fight on to the end."

A shiver ran down Stanley's spine, a shiver that rippled a hundredfold down the ranks of listening men. The wireless was switched off and an address was made.

"All active dog sections are to be sent up to the Front, every last man and every last dog. To go straight up with no delay. The dogs are in urgent demand. Go forward and honor the reputation your work has already earned."

The waiting men grouped into their units for specific instructions. Stanley's orders were to return immediately to the Villers-Bretonneux sector.

"You, Ryder, will be reporting to Captain James McManus, at the Brigade HQ Signal Station. Captain McManus has specifically requested you. The Captain's Station is assigned to Brigadier-General Glasgow's Thirteenth Brigade of the Fourth Australian Division. A critical action is expected at Villers. Aerial observations show enemy troops massing by Hangard Wood, about a mile south of the town. The Hun has resupplied his troops, brought his big guns up, put six fresh divisions on his front. The lie of the land in your sector is awkward. A steep north-facing slope leads up to the Signal Station. They're experiencing heavy losses among the runners—there's cover going down, but no cover for the runners who have to come up. Do your best, Ryder—we're under orders to hold the Somme at all costs. Remember—if Villers falls, Amiens falls. If Amiens falls, Paris falls."

Stanley was in turmoil. Paris and Amiens meant nothing to him. Tom was coming and even if Tom were to beg his brother to go home, still Stanley ached to see him.

"One more for you, Ryder," came a shout from the Post Office.

A card this time, not a letter—Cross Post—the inter-Army post—stamped the 13th, the day before yesterday, and two inverted YMCA triangles—Tom! Another letter from Tom! Stanley read.

I'm instructed straight for the Amiens area, not to stop at Etaples where I had hoped to find you. I hope you are not in the Amiens section. Things are not going well for us there and the enemy continues to bring in more men. I am terrified for you, Stanley, I am torn between wanting you to leave and wanting you to stay so that I see you. Lara continues to look for Da. We must both pray that she finds him safe.

In great haste, Tom.

Cross Post only took twenty-four hours within any single Army area: Tom could be anywhere up here—might be here now—heading like Stanley himself for the Amiens area. Where was he? There were different stamps for each Field Post Office—but this stamp was just a number and didn't mean anything to him. Which division was he joining? Which brigade, which corps?

Stanley whirled around, searching the convoys and vehicles and trains of departing men. A battalion of Australians, wearing brown slouch hats and broad smiles, marched along the dusty road in the distance with a quick swaggering step to the beat of a pipe band.

"Well, God help Jerry," breathed the postal orderly who'd given Stanley his mail. Stanley looked at the Anzacs, saw their smiles, watched them pass and pass in endless ranks, their buttons and badges winking and flashing in the pale evening light, saw each smiling face, each ready to fight to the end.

Stanley saw them, and knew they had to go back up, he and Pistol, and do the work they'd been trained to do. Tom would find Stanley later. In the meantime they were under orders and had a duty to James and Hamish.

Next morning, squeezed once again into the corner of a dark cattle truck, Field Marshal Haig's words echoed uneasily in Stanley's head: "Every position must be held to the last man . . . each one of us must fight on to the end."

While they were waiting at an intersection in the road, a machine-gun limber pulled by a team of twelve horses, all bay, passed by. Da's preference had always been for bays; he said they took less cleaning. As always, Stanley searched the team of horses in case there was a Thornley horse among them. No, he told himself, a good Thornley horse would be a prize cavalry horse. Trumpet, though, the old cob, would, in his day, have made a good limber horse . . .

Stanley felt a lurch in his gut as he remembered Da whipping Trumpet so violently there at the edge of the lake, when Da had wanted to race away and avoid his son. It was odd, Stanley thought, his thoughts veering from Trumpet, that Da had taken the trap. He wondered why he hadn't thought of this before. Was he seeing things more clearly now that the horror of losing Soldier had ebbed, that his feelings toward Da had grown blurry and confused?

He marched onward, Pistol trotting airily at his heels, but Stanley's unease about the trap grew and tangled itself around his whole being. Where had Da gone that morning, and why?

Misgivings and fears still gnawed away at Stanley as his unit halted at the entrance to a communication trench and stood waiting under the hot sun. He jumped out of his skin as his hand touched a wooden cross. There was a cluster of them to his left that he hadn't noticed. Stanley moved away towards the duckboard track and the sign saying "WALK-ING WOUNDED." Four weeks ago he'd marched up to the Front, only to be greeted by Hunter's ridicule. Corporal Hunter. Stanley glanced toward the crosses, wondering.

He called Pistol aside to allow passage to a Subaltern with a wounded arm and bright white sling. "Good luck, sir," Stanley whispered.

Without turning or raising his head, the Subaltern grunted, "It's you as wants the good luck, I'm out of here."

They reached the end of the communication trench. A group of the Black Watch trailed forward, white knees glowing beneath dark kilts. To one side of the duckboard track stood a Lance-Corporal with a group of tired, sweat-streaked, blood-soaked men, groundsheets across their shoulders. He held a sheaf of papers calling out names, one after another. "Fraser," he called, waited, then called again, "Fraser." A third time he called the name. When there was again no answer, he scored out the name with a single stroke.

The back line ran in front of Villers and across two valleys, one leading to the banks of the River Somme to the north, the other to the south and the River Luce, Stanley's guide said. As Stanley made his way along, the friendly Australians smiled at him, greeted Pistol. They had a good reputation at Central Kennels for liking dogs.

All along the line, vast preparations were afoot, convoys of goods being ferried in both directions, while the entire front line, from the wood that was at forward right to the Roman road at forward left leading to Villers, flickered with the distant flashes of firing guns. The slope running up to the ridge along which Stanley's trench ran had valleys whose clefts and gullies would help an enemy creeping up to fight for the high ground. The runners would be having a bad time of it; this slope was a dangerous business.

"Captain McManus, sir?" said Stanley as he entered the Brigade Signal Station and looked around with interest. It was larger and better equipped than Hunter's station. James stepped forward and put an arm around Stanley's shoulder. There, too, was Hamish. In another corner, by the Fuller-phone, was Fidget, curled up next to his basket of pigeons—untidily, like a straggling towel. It was good to see him, too. James, though warm and welcoming, was brief with Stanley, a little tense, and returned quickly to the Fuller-phone, but Fidget and Hamish led Stanley to his new funk-hole.

Evening, 23 April 1918

Aquenne Wood, near Cachy

Two days passed. More men arrived, more ammunition, more provisions. The certainty of an attack being ordered grew with each new convoy. At Rations-Up, the messenger had a letter for Stanley. It was from Cross Post again, this time in a Church Army envelope, addressed in an elegant and precise hand Stanley didn't recognize, but which he thought might be Father Bill's—that at last he'd traced Tom. Since Stanley, too, now knew where Tom was, he took it back with him to his funk-hole to read after tea.

Étaples
22 April 1918

Dear Stanley,
I hope this finds you safe and well. I
am sorry to take so long.
  As you know, Tom is serving with
the East Lancashires. At the time
of writing this, he has returned from
leave and is instructed to join the 8th
Division in the Amiens area. More than
that I am not able to tell you.

Stanley started: the 8th Division? That was *this* sector. Part of the 8th Division lay in reserve and part in the front lines. Where would Tom be?

While searching for your brother, I
found another Ryder, one that you were,
perhaps, not expecting to find here: your
father, Dixon Ryder.

Stanley leaped up, dumbfounded, his heart racing. Da?
No!

> *Your father is serving with the Remounts — horse provisioning for the cavalry.*

Da was too old, surely? The Remounts didn't take men of
his age. How old was he? Younger than he looked; fifty,
perhaps. Lara Bird's father had signed up—perhaps they
were taking old men now. Stanley spun around to the
parados—the rear side of the trench—as though amid the
carts and limbers and troops on the move he might see Da's
white head.

> *His unit arrived at Etaples last week.
> I sought him out and told him you
> were also in this sector — that I'd seen
> you.*

Etaples? Stanley had an overwhelming impulse to abandon his post, to run and run, to search every crack and crevice of France till he found Da, to hear the truth from Da's own lips about Soldier.

He treated me to a robust explosion of colorful language, most of which cannot be repeated by a clergyman, but which stemmed, I think, only from fear for your safety. He is beside himself with worry for you and, if he doesn't find you first, he will write to you and ask you to return home.

Things will never be the same again for any of us here. When you return, you may find you feel a stranger even to yourself. If you find it so, Stanley, do not also be a stranger to your family. You have a father who dearly loves you, who would follow you to the end of the world.

God bless and keep you safe,
Father Bill.

Stanley was standing on quicksand, everything shifting around him. Whatever, he thought, whatever was done or not done, Da was out here because he'd come to find Stanley.

The Remounts. There were 500,000 horses on the Western Front. Stanley smiled. That would keep Da busy. Busy and proud again, proud to be doing the work he loved. Da knew as much about horses as any man, more than any man. Still awash with uncertainties, Stanley sat waiting with Pistol. The tangle of weeds on the parapet glowed a violent yellow against the ominous gunmetal sky.

Two hours later he was still waiting for the man who would collect Pistol, the sky now wild and sinister, lashed with streaks of violet and wine.

Hamish! That was Hamish coming, his familiar bulk filling the height and width of the trench. Hamish greeted Pistol—he always greeted Pistol by way of greeting Stanley.

"Aye, you're a good 'un. A cracker of a dog. The laddie's doing you some good, and you're doing him no harm either, I'm thinking." He tousled the dog's ears. "An' I'm as likely to get an answer out of you as your master." Hamish smiled at Stanley and rose, and they stood together looking up at the sky through the camouflage netting.

Hamish sniffed the air, like a hound. "I don't like the look of that sky one wee bit," he said. "There's rain in it, round rain." Hamish looked down to the scorched plain below. "Tens of thousands of men, Stanley, hiding, like rats. In every crack of this plain. Moved here like pawns from every corner of the globe. Tomorrow she'll give up her men, spew thousands of tons of steel from her very guts—"

Hamish was interrupted by an infantryman who'd approached from behind.

"Keeper Ryder?"

Hamish's serious face softened with a comforting, crinkly smile.

"He's here, laddie, to take your wee dog away."

Stanley steeled himself for a brave and brief goodbye.

"Come back safe, Pistol. Come back safe." He handed the lead to the infantryman. "Look after him, sir."

As Pistol turned the corner up to the access branch, his long snout doubled back along his spine toward Stanley, his tail whirring.

"Stand-to is at three," said Hamish. "Zero hour is three thirty. Goodnight, laddie."

He frowned at the sinister sky once more, and left.

Dawn, 24 April 1918

Aquenne Wood, near Cachy

At 3 a.m., all the way along the front line, as far as Stanley could see, the men of the 13th Brigade stood to on the fire step. He heard too the time-bomb tick-tick-tick of Fidget's watch.

A platoon leader brought the rum ration around in a two-gallon stone jar. "Open up, open up," he said to each man.

His pulse throbbing like a drum, Stanley took the rum for the first time, hoping to still his pounding heart, but it burned his throat and took his breath away.

Haloes of luminous mist cradled the hollows and crevices of the plain. A whispered word of warning flew like wind along the trench. Stanley's blood ran cold, fear for himself and fear for Pistol compounded into one.

At three thirty, platoon leaders up and down the front line blew their whistles. The Australians climbed over their parapets, bayonets fixed. Stanley scrabbled for his own bay-onet, to poke a hole in the breastwork of the trench, boring like a worm through wood, a rivulet of sand spilling down the parapet wall. Like the gunners, he could now see with-out raising his head above the parapet. Eye to the hole, he saw buff and grey and blue lines of men bursting the bounds of trenches he didn't even know were there—to the right the French blue, directly ahead the Australian buff and some English khaki, together, guns raised, bayonets fixed, a flood of men, advancing in silence.

Behind the wave of attacking riflemen followed four signalers, two carrying a wire on a reel, paying it out as they went, two others carrying lamps, phones, and spare wires. The wires would run from the posts the advancing signalers hoped to set up back to the Signal Station.

The heavy guns burst into fire.

"Three thousand howitzers—we've got three thousand howitzers along this front!" yelled Fidget, his voice round with pride.

The howitzers flashed and blazed, firing shells that screeched like a vast tearing of linen in tremendous arcs across the sky, leaving red shooting-star trails till, at the top of their arc, they dipped and flashed red in a distant boom.

"They're forming a barrage—a barrage of fire, to move along in front of the infantry—to protect them." Fidget gestured to the horrifying, terrifying continuous arc of flame that ran for as far north as Stanley could see—perhaps ten miles long. Fidget laughed happily.

"We caught him sleeping. Jerry was sleeping."

At four Jerry opened up, and now every gun in the world was firing, the earth upheaving, the whole horizon alight. So long as everything went well, so long as the lines held, then there'd be no need for Pistol. "Keep advancing, hold the line, keep advancing," the boy prayed, his mouth dry with fear. "Hold the line and Pistol will be OK."

You could no longer tell whose shells were whose. Between the smoke and the mist Stanley couldn't see more than twenty-five yards ahead, could only see flares and flames, explosions, stabs and flashes of colored light. Cordite filled the air and drifted toward him. The whistles and shrieks of shells, the roar of the artillery, the swishing of bullets all mingled into one tremendous, continuous roar so that his eardrums tore with infernal, maddening noise that seemed to come from both within and without.

The world was breaking into pieces, Stanley's heart jumping as chunks of earth and rock and splinters leaped into the air. Pieces of stone and lumps of earth as big—bigger than—a man were falling like hail. Shells burst with a bluish hue, ripping the earth apart, spewing hundreds and hundreds of tons of earth skyward, turning the country into a mass of crawling flame, killing any feeling inside him other than fear for Pistol.

"Four miles—that's a four-mile frontage—the enemy's replying over four miles," shouted Fidget into Stanley's ear. "They want Villers . . ."

There was a new jumpiness in Fidget's fraying exhilaration, an excessive mobility in his face, in his fluttering fingers. Had Fidget spent too long at the Front? He'd had no leave, Stanley knew, had returned immediately to the Front after leaving Stanley and Bones at the ambulance.

To Stanley's right a sudden, horrifying cliff of fire rose up, shades of green and brown and grey, all fused together. That was the front line surely—was enemy fire falling now behind the front lines? There to the right—was it falling behind the front line to Stanley's right? There—just where

Stanley had been watching, a Very light went up. That white magnesium blaze was the Allies' SOS signal. Something was wrong up there on the right, where clouds of smoke bellowed out and shooting tongues of flame licked the sky. How could the lines of communication hold when the bowels of the earth were open? And if the lines failed, what then? They'd not send a dog, surely, into such an inferno?

At a quarter to five a feeble dawn began to creep across the battlefield. Not a bird had risen to greet the day. The Front was being very heavily shelled, the earth beneath Stanley shaking like a jelly, the air trembling and boiling. Seismic quavering rippled to the edge of the trench, triggering cascades of earth over his helmet. What was happening? Where was Pistol? Had the bombardment moved closer? Was it aiming for the reserve lines? It was impossible to see what was going on; the enemy might be putting down a smoke barrage. Stanley's eyes ached and stung.

The heavens finally cracked. A thunderstorm crashed and rolled across the plain. Rain pounded and hammered the earth. Very lights soared like shooting stars above the Allied lines, flaring against the glistening curtains of rain. Things were going very badly.

Would Pistol be sent out into *this*? Was Tom out *there*? For a few seconds, Stanley closed his eyes, then turned away. The unbearable fear, the noise and the fear together, might fracture him, split him in two. It was beyond bearing; he must think of something else to fight it off. There—Stanley bent to the streaming wall of the parapet: a crowd of staghorn beetles trotting up and down. That chalky soil, turned slippery in the rain, was now just the place for a stag-horn. They'd appeared with the rain, hordes of them, with their armored bodies and antler-type mandibles. The stegosaurus of beetles. Beetles, Stanley remembered, were everywhere, in every niche on earth, from the most arid desert to the swampiest wetland. Everywhere except Antarctica.

Hamish had come up from below and was looking over the top. Stanley shrugged off his raincoat and held it over the two of them to shelter them from the rain that battered down through the netting cover.

"We'll never see anything like this again—never. It's the largest artillery bombardment any of us will surely ever see," bellowed Hamish.

"Are the lines holding?" Stanley shouted back.

"Aye . . . so far . . . so far they're holding . . . but Villers is surrounded by enemy machine guns on the north, west, and south. Amiens is under direct observation. The Hun's got a pocket four miles wide and one mile deep around Villers"—Hamish gestured toward the two groups of trees to the north-east, barely discernible—"and parts of Monument and Hangard Woods."

There were shouts from the Signal Station, panic and pandemonium below.

"A Company gone!"

Hamish leaped away down the steps.

"B Company gone!"

"C Company OK!"

"Message from C Company. We are surrounded, sir, what do we do?"

Was Pistol with C Company?

Two linesmen rushed out and scuttled over the top, crawling like rats, forward and downward in the drenching rain.

"C Company gone!"

Hamish rushed up the stairs and along the trench, stern and grey, his coat running with water like a Highland waterfall. He put his eye to the telescope. A few seconds passed.

"All gone. All dead." There was disbelief in his voice. "No communication with the front line."

Stanley held his helmet over the lens to keep off the rain.

"Dead!" Hamish said again. "All of them, one by one, all dead."

The linesmen were slithering onward. Stanley watched them, shaking and horrified. It was impossible, surely, under such rain, such fire, to find and repair the ends of wires, but he still prayed. "Find the ends. Please find the ends of the wires. Don't let them send Pistol."

Hamish swung the telescope back and forth, back and forth along the horizon. "C Company sur-rounded . . . All forward visual stations . . . destroyed. All gone. All lines of communication down." He turned aghast to Stanley. "We've nothing, no communication with the front line." Hamish shook his head in horror. "No semaphore. No signal lamp. Pigeons. Nothing in this—" he gestured to the rain. "They can't send for artillery support, can't SOS . . . Nothing . . ."

"Wh-where is he? Is Pistol with C Company?"

Hamish paused and looked shocked for a second. Then he turned and, as though talking to an uncomprehending child, said gently, "No, laddie. B—he's with B Company."

Hamish left, and Stanley stood under the pounding rain, eardrums tearing with the unending noise. To his forward

179

right, the Allied lines looked thin and confused. No more than a brigade here and a brigade there. The church tower, on the vulnerable spur of the plateau jutting out to the west, was smoldering. What was happening? Where was Fidget? Fidget would know. Had the front line broken? Were men pulling back? Where was Pistol?

Still the drenching rain thundered on. The ditches had stretched out into glistening bogs, the intricate lacework of the streams blocked by the shelling, the ground turned to a quagmire. Soaked to the marrow, a stream of water pouring off the back of his helmet and down his neck, Stanley saw figures dribbling back from the front line, from the wood known as the Monument, stumbling and sinking in the soupy ground.

Everything was wringing wet. The sump ditch had over-flown, the trench, already puddled, filled steadily. There was a frog on the duckboards. Funny how the frogs didn't mind the shelling but the mice had the wind up and had gone underground. If he could only stop his legs shaking, his fingers, his heart shaking, Stanley thought, he could focus his field glasses on that shell hole below, the closest one, and there'd be more frogs, marsh frogs probably, ten or twenty of them in that. Trigger, wherever he was, would be amused by the marsh frogs.

Captain McManus came up.

"Where's the dog? Is he not in? Please God they'll have sent the dog . . . They've nothing else . . ." He started and clutched Stanley. "Look, Stanley—he's here—he's in—he's in . . ."

Stanley leaped. There—in the confusion of smoke and

fog and the glistening curtain of rain, was Pistol, racing like a silver shadow across the greedy, gleaming morass, skimming it as easily and lightly as a bird. There was that long grey head, the commonplace dog with the laughing eyes. Stanley spun on a Catherine wheel of love and pride.

There was the sudden screech of a heavy shell.

"Run, Pistol, run . . . *run*," breathed Stanley.

The shell dipped at its arc and crashed to the ground some forty feet below Pistol. The ground beneath Stanley shook and rattled, the earth of the parapet cascaded down, but the dog never so much as flinched—was still running onward.

"What a dog, laddie, what a dog!"

Stanley pulled aside the sodden, battered Queen Anne's lace on the parapet to see, then yanked aside the camouflage, ready for Pistol, feeling for the titbit in his pocket, watching with bated breath as the dog leaped over the fire step and, in a single fluid motion, sat, breathless, tongue loose, panting, grinning, panting, grinning. There was something about this dog, this nondescript dog he'd once thought he'd never love, something in those laughing eyes, that gripped Stanley's heartstrings now like a vice. Stanley knew, at this moment, and with total certainty, that he must never, ever lose him.

Stanley's hands trembled as he unscrewed the cylinder. He noted the time of departure given on the note—9.30 a.m.— and handed the message to James.

"Good boy, good." Stanley fed Pistol the canned beef. James bent and patted Pistol, then, sheltering under Stanley's raincoat, glanced at the note and checked his watch.

"Nine thirty-seven. I salute your dog, Keeper Ryder. Nearly

four miles in seven minutes." James looked down. "From B Company," he said, then read aloud so Stanley could hear. "Front-line companies, Second East Lancs and Second West Yorks forced back from the Monument to the north, to railway station, making our way westward along railway line to north-east corner of Aquenne Wood. Enemy troops have taken Villers and Monument, and infiltrating the Aquenne Wood from the Monument. All signalers in forward Signal Stations killed or captured. All lines of communication down. Remains of Yorks and Lancs are surrounded in the Monument, have no ammunition, no supplies. German position attacking not known. Further attacks expected."

Stanley looked up at James. The East Lancs? Tom—was he with them, surrounded and with no supplies? "Infiltrating the Aquenne"? Coming here? He clutched at James's coat.

"The East Lancs?"

But James had already turned, was hurling himself down the steps to the Signal Station shouting, "They'll be decimated!"

The field glasses were streaming—Stanley must wipe them, but his hands were wet, his coat sodden. Men were pouring along the communication trench to Stanley's right, crowding into the intersection beyond Fidget's hole, collecting in the back lines—men with no puttees and torn tunics. There were shouts that the right flank was coming back in disarray.

Somewhere an officer bellowed, "Retreat! Retreat! Turn round and run like blazes!"

There was shooting in all directions.

"Take cover! Take cover!"

"Collect Mills bombs, arm yourselves. Keep moving backwards. Take up position one hundred yards back." Stanley's parapet was whipped by a hailstorm of bullets. Everyone was down on all fours in the sump water of the trench. By Fidget's hole, men were yelling and firing. In the division of the trench beyond Fidget was a shaft crowded with wounded men, helpless and immobile, a jumble of men of all stripes.

"Move on! Move on!"

There was a screech. The earth of the parapet spewed up. Dirt rained over Stanley in avalanches. Showers of mud and metal collapsed the roof netting, shells pinging as they hit the corrugated iron cover of the Signal Station.

"Move on, move on!"

To Stanley's left, the artillerymen collected on the fire step and leaped down into the stream of wounded men, keeping low, half crawling along the duckboards.

"Down the trench. Down the trench."

Stanley hesitated. Where were the signalers? What would James's instructions be? He forced his way against the flood of men, toward the Signal Station, knowing without looking that Pistol would be at his heels. Bullets whistled and screeched overhead. There was James on the stairs to the Station. Behind him followed a caterpillar of signalers, runners, a trench mortar officer, the wireless operator—all mud-smeared, lugging boxes, cables, tables, the Fuller-phone, emerging, blinking into the light like strange, earth-dwelling slugs.

At the far end of the straight bay, the Australian Brigadier-General was running against the flow of crawling men, yelling at them.

"Get up and get into place and I'll tell you when to take cover. Stay in your place!"

Hamish thrust a Lee-Enfield rifle into Stanley's hands. "Fix the bayonet."

Stanley fixed the bayonet and rotated it. He was in the front line; would have to defend himself—to kill, if necessary. He slid the bayonet abruptly into its housing over the barrel.

"If you need tae, drive that toothpick as far home as you can. Aye, and twist it too, before you pull it out—It's him or you, and for my sake, make sure it's him."

There were more shouts.

"Stay where you are and hold the line!"

"You're going into action at once!"

Stanley was pushed aside as another rush of men—not Australians, these, but men in English khaki—came over the fire step and plunged along the trench. Was that the red rose of the East Lancs on those collar badges? Were they men of Tom's battalion?

Abandoning the bayonet, Stanley rushed after them. Were they Lancashires? Leaping and dodging, he forced his way downstream through the rush of men with Pistol at his heels, weightless and agile as a shadow. The last of the Lancashires, the one at the back—that one! That last one was Tom's height and build. Stanley ran, shouting frantically, "Tom! Tom!"

No one turned or stopped.

"Tom!" Stanley called again, scrambling through men. He reached the intersection and snatched at the back of a coat, missed, and snatched again at a sleeve.

"Tom Ryder. Was he with you? Tom Ryder?" The soldier rushed on, and Stanley felt, where an arm should be, only a fraying cuff which disintegrated in his hands. He opened his palm and saw shreds of bloodied cloth. Too desperate to compass the man's wound, Stanley ran on, caught another man by the shoulders, and made him turn.

"Sir, sir, was Tom Ryder with you? Do you know Tom Ryder?"

The man looked at Stanley, his eyes glassy with fear. "Yes, he's out there, cut off in the Monument. What's left of C Company is up there with what's left of the Second West Yorks. Brave, your Tom Ryder—held Jerry up with a revolver, kept on shooting, on and on, gave his men time to pull sandbags into place. There's a machine gun on them somewhere, snipers on them everywhere, they're sitting ducks— no ammunition, can't get a message out, the Signal Station is blown to bits." He shook his head, turned and moved on.

Stanley leaped up the nearest fire step, straining to see the group of trees he knew to be the Monument. Everything was quiet there. Behind him, someone was shouting, "Retire and get the lads back! Get the lads back!"

Stanley forced his way upstream against the flow of men, back to his post. With trembling, mud-clogged hands, he grabbed his field glasses, and again scanned the ring of trees around the plain.

The Brigadier-General was back, walking along the trench. His voice was calm and slow.

"Stay where you are. Hold the line. Company Commanders to assemble at the double. We're in the most advanced position. The enemy's broken through on our immediate front. It's through and past us on the right flank."

Fidget was huddled on Stanley's platform, next to his

pigeon basket. Sodden strands of straw-colored hair clung to Fidget's streaming forehead, his gaunt face a picture of alarm, fog, and confusion in his watery eyes. The day had perhaps been too much for him. His eyes skittered and his mouth was helter-skelter as he said, "We'll never get out . . . never get out . . ."

Stanley gave an irritated shake of the shoulders. "We're better off than the men in the Aquenne. Would you rather be there?"

"Stay where you are. Hold the line. Stay where you are. Hold the line . . ."

An hour passed while officers collected stragglers and noncombatants. Men of all stripes were armed, anyone who could still hold a rifle—tailors, grooms, buglers, officer's batmen, even Cook. Fidget and Stanley waited in line, with bayonets fixed. They were given a dry biscuit, then stretched out into a skeleton battle formation.

The rain was lighter now. Stanley could see where the line, to the left, was scattered and broken, manned by an exhausted ragtag battalion. The English 8th Division in the front line was overwhelmed, had sustained losses beyond endurance. The medical services were overwhelmed, and in the shaft beyond Fidget, wounded Lancs and Yorks were being patched up by their own comrades.

Hamish and the sappers, under Captain McManus's direction, were setting up equipment in Stanley's dug-out, building a new forward Signal Station. Stanley, eyes straying helplessly toward the Monument, was supposed to be rigging up the Aldis lamp.

"There'll be a counterattack," said Hamish grimly. "The

generals won't let Amiens fall, won't let Villers stay in German hands. There's no option for them. Sooner or later, there's going to be a counterattack."

Pistol half sat, half crouched, trying to keep his haunches above the sump water of the trench, never taking his eyes off Stanley. An iron roof was dragged over the trench, men hauled up reels of cable, looped wires around the walls, and set up the instruments. Looking up from his polishing of the lamp's lens, Stanley saw the grey dog raise his head too. He saw the dog's unexceptional looks and he saw in his solemn eyes the wise and loyal soul within. Hamish, too, watched as Pistol's nose followed Stanley's hands as they coiled the wire of the lamp, and said, "By any measure, that dog is more, laddie, than a dog."

Early afternoon, 24 April 1918

Aquenne Wood, near Cachy

Stanley looked, for the thousandth time, to the north-west, to the shards of trees that clawed the sky like desperate fingerless hands.

A Brigade Commander appeared with new staff, all fresh and clean.

"We must counterattack at once. B Company will be in the center, C Company will take the right. Get ready. There's no time to waste."

There was disbelief and resignation in the faces of the infantrymen, exhaustion in their slumped bodies, but once again they readied themselves for an inspection and waited for what might have been an hour. There were more shouts, a patrol, waiting, more waiting, more shouts, another patrol.

For another hour nothing happened. The rain exhausted itself. Disagreements within the High Command filtered down as counter-commands.

"Stay where you are. Hold the line. There'll be no attack."

A Lieutenant-Colonel appeared. "You're going into action at once."

He was met by a Brigadier-General with a rugged and honest face.

"Brigadier-General Glasgow," whispered Fidget.

"All our artillery is out of action and the enemy has all his guns in position. We'll be annihilated by the machine-gun emplacements in the Monument if we try to attack." The Brigadier-General's voice was deep and calm, his Australian accent exotic and strange to Stanley. "If it was God Almighty who gave the order, we wouldn't do it in daylight." It was good, thought Stanley, to be commanded by such a man.

In the mid afternoon the sun appeared fully. Stanley's sodden uniform began to steam. The sump water of the trench gave out a rank sweat.

Had Tom escaped? Stanley raised his field glasses and scanned the maze of ridges and pits below, seeing only shovels, water bottles, tin hats, maps, flares, stretchers, gas cans, beef tins, and groundsheets. Was Tom out there, washed up amid the relics of things that had once been? Stanley saw a figure wriggling, like a worm, out of one shell hole into another. The man didn't stand a chance, couldn't even steady a gun in that mud.

For the moment there was to be no attack, the High Command still arguing among itself, the Australians refusing to obey English orders to counterattack in daylight. Some sort of rations had come up and a line was forming by Cook. Cook must be relieved, Stanley thought, to put down his bayonet and find himself back in charge of his kitchen. Stanley stayed where he was, his thoughts still with Tom, with Da, his fingers worrying at Pistol's ears.

Fidget appeared, holding his army biscuits in one hand, in the other a letter. Fidget handed over the biscuits, then, as a thing of infinitely lesser value, the letter. Stanley saw the stamp "ON ACTIVE SERVICE" along the top, saw the stilted hand on the envelope—Da. His heart racing, his palms sweaty, he saw the APO S11 stamp: Cross Mail, the stamp of the Stationary Field Post Office at Etaples—Da was still at Etaples! Stanley took a deep breath, opened the envelope, unfolded the sheet, saw the careful letters and the hand that had labored over the unwilling words. Warily, he began to read.

> Etaples
> 22 April 1918
>
> Stanley,
> He's here, Stanley, your dog is here.

Out here? Had Da taken leave of his senses? Had he not—? Soldier not dead—out here? Alive and out here? Stanley raced on.

> I did you wrong when I took him to the Dogs Home in Liverpool, but I have tried since then to put that wrong right and I pray you will find it in your heart to forgive me.

Stanley gulped and froze. Da hadn't done it, he'd never done it—he'd taken Soldier to the Home, hadn't drowned him—Soldier was alive—where? Stanley charged on, scrambling and tripping over words.

> When Ma died, I missed her so much that every single other thing in the world was blotted out. I hope that you will never suffer as I did. And although I pray that you will never yourself know the frame of mind which can drive a man to a desperate act, I hope you will one day, be it many years away, understand that grief can drive a good man to terrible deeds. I did want to drown your dog, Stanley, God forgive me, I did want to, but I never did.

Where is he, Da? Tell me where he is.

When I found you gone I went to get him
back but they told me he'd cut loose
from the Home that first morning and
hadn't been found since. A week later
they wrote to tell me that he'd been
picked up as a stray and recruited as
a War Dog. They sent him out here, son.
His collar reads WAR MESSENJER DOG
NUMBER 2176.

2176? Stanley's heart vaulted—blue twos and ones and sev-
ens and sixes shimmered and jumped on the white page.
With fumbling fingers, Stanley clutched at Pistol's collar—he knew the number—but—no—something was wrong—
Pistol was 2176. Stanley stared at the tag. The digits leaped
and jumped and disordered themselves. Stanley's fingers
released the tag. Stanley began to shake. 2176, *Pistol* was
2176. Feverish and clumsy, Stanley took up the letter. 2176
it said—Da was wrong—had got the number wrong—*Pistol*
was 2176. Stanley turned from the letter to the collar again
and looked, still uncomprehending, into Pistol's troubled
eyes. Stanley caught his breath—those dark eyes—his gut
lurching with doubt and shock and wondrous hope—those
eyes . . . Was it possible—were they Soldier's? The milky pup
he'd held in the palm of his hand, the tiny bundle Rocket
had dropped on his lap—was it possible?—Could he have
grown so tall? Soldier would be five months now, almost
six—Soldier's tripping, coltish legs—had they grown so long,

so fast? Stanley held fistfuls of Pistol's grey coat. Was this Soldier's—had the porridge deepened to silver?

Tears streaming down his cheeks, Stanley caught at Soldier's ears, his tail, his legs, in a fever of amazement.

"Soldier," he choked. "You knew, didn't you?" With bemused and narrowed laughing eyes, Soldier opened his jaws and grinned back at Stanley. "You knew as soon as you saw me, you've known all along, but I, I didn't . . ."

Stanley threw himself on Soldier, held the whole dog in his arms, rocking him back and forth, a sunburst of wonder and warmth erupting in the wounded center of his heart, unraveling its dark knot of grief. Adrift and weightless on a surge of joy, Stanley leaned back against the sandbag, pulling the dog closer, breathing the warm wet smell of his coat, feeling the quiet tears on his own cheeks.

"Was it me," he asked, "me that you were trying to find when you broke free from the home?"

Soldier's tail flipped to and fro with pleasure at his master's sudden and unexpected show of affection. That feathery tail and coat—that was the Laxton dog in Soldier, that was Jake, the hound Stanley had met on Rocky Brow the afternoon he'd lost Rocket; but Soldier's lightness and speed were all Rocket's.

Holding Da's letter behind Soldier's head, Stanley read on.

I am out here to find you both – both
son and dog. Stanley, it was a fault of
mine that drove you away from home but
I pray I may find your dog and return
him to you, and would give everything to
know you are both safe at Thornley.
The clergyman, Father Bill, tells me
that your work with the Signallers is
behind the front lines and I am grateful
for that but I pray that you will go
home and, God willing, I will join you
there.
Da.

"God willing"? What had Stanley done? He stared with
blurred eyes at the rumpled, trembling sheet. Drips fell
through the trench cover, splodging the ink. Da was out
here.

Stanley swung from the dizzy tiptop of joy to the hollows
of fear. What had he done?

"Da must go home, Soldier, this is no place for Da." Stanley leaped up. "He shouldn't be here. We must find him, tell
him we can all go home now."

What did the boy want? Soldier's arched, flickering brows
asked.

"We must find Da and we must take him home."

194

His mind racing, Stanley snatched up his pack, clipped a lead on Soldier. He'd tell James that he and Soldier were leaving.

They reached the steps to the Signal Station and Stanley came abruptly face to face with Captain McManus. Behind him stood Hamish, the pair of them filling the height and width of the trench, men born to larger lands, to deeper valleys, and steeper hills than these.

"Oh no," breathed Stanley and began to shake his head firmly and slowly from side to side.

Holding Stanley's gaze, the Captain's blue eyes were worried, his face grim and drawn.

"No," said Stanley. "No. I can't. I have to find my father." The Captain didn't hear, was speaking at the same time.

"Keeper Ryder, we've got to make contact with the men in the Monument. We've got to clear the enemy machine-gun positions there before we can counter-attack. Prepare your dog. I'm sending him up by the route under the canal."

Hamish stepped forward and put a gentle hand on Stanley's shoulder. Stanley shook his head.

"No."

The Captain stepped closer, lowered his voice, and said urgently, "Stanley, only the men in the Monument know the enemy positions. We've got to get a message back from them. I can get a runner out there, but I can't get him back up the slope. There's no cover, it's too exposed from below."

"No. I must find my father."

"Stanley, I've no choice. Your dog is our only hope."

You have no choice, but I do, thought Stanley. "No," he said, shaking his head again, "I cannot lose this dog, he cannot go." Stanley's words were firm and strong, no dryness, no stammer. "No," he said again. When the Captain replied, there was anguish in his voice.

"We lost ten runners, Stanley. Ten." Behind Hamish, Stanley saw an Australian infantryman waiting. Stanley glanced out over the parapet. Send Soldier? He spun around.

"No," he said again. "No."

The Captain bent forward and hissed, "They're sitting ducks till they get a message back with the position of the machine guns. Keeper Ryder, the Lancs have no other hope."

The Lancs. Stanley recoiled as the full agony of his position hit him. Without Soldier's message, Tom and the men in the Monument could not be saved. Stanley was to lose either a brother or a dog.

"I'll go. I'll go. Don't send the dog, send me."

James gave an exasperated shake of his head, stood tall, and said in a sharp, clipped voice, "I have no other option, and *you*, Keeper Ryder, have a duty and will obey my order."

Hamish intercepted gently.

"You have no choice, Stanley. The dog must go."

With mingled fear and horror, Stanley turned to Soldier. He saw Soldier's watchful, flickering brows, his liquid eyes, swishing tail, the poised and ready foreleg. Stanley bowed his head, knelt in the sump water of the trench, held the long grey head, and said, "Bring me a message from Tom . . . but . . . come back . . . just come back." With a strangled sound, he added, "Go, boy. Go," as he held out the lead to the waiting infantryman.

Two hours later

Aquenne Wood

There in that desolate huddle of trees were two of the three beings Stanley most loved.

On Soldier's safe return depended Tom's life, and the life of Soldier himself. On Soldier's safe return depended too the fate of Villers, the fate of Amiens, and of Paris. How strange that the events of Stanley's own life, the beat of his own heart, should pound in such precise collision with the pulse of the War.

Hamish, his face lit in a shaft of amber sun, remained at Stanley's side. His eyes were resting on Da's letter. "Your father?"

Stanley nodded.

"He didnae know, did he, your father? Didnae know you were here?"

Stanley shook his head. "No," he said.

"Stanley, this is nae place for you . . . even with the Dog Service."

"No," Stanley burst out. "This is no place for dogs, or horses, no place for sons or fathers or brothers. But until I'd read Da's letter, there was no other place for me." Hamish stretched an arm around Stanley's shoulder. A little while passed. When Stanley was calmer, he said, "My brother . . . he's out there, with the East Lancs."

"Oh, laddie . . ."

Hamish was silent as together they both looked out over the parapet, their eyes tracing the route Soldier might run, out of the wood, across a marshy, shelterless belt of land, over the canal, and then up the steep slope, leading to the trench in which they stood.

"So much, Stanley, depends on your dog"—Hamish shook his head doubtfully—"Jerry's all around and everywhere—you can't say where he is and where he isn't." He was putting the field glasses back to his eyes again when the wary quiet of the twilight was shattered by a sudden splutter of machine-gun fire, a savage shriek, from the right of the Bois.

A volcano of earth and debris erupted in the Monument. Closer, there was a splutter of machine-gun fire—but from where? Farther down the trench where the Devon infantry stood, a shout went up. Fidget appeared out of nowhere, gripping Stanley—something was there in the far distance, hurtling low and fast toward the canal. You couldn't see a dog at all, just a grey blur, a silver streak. Hamish was yelling for James; Stanley was measuring the land the dog had to cover, the distance, the minutes it might take. Twelve perhaps. Twelve; if Soldier kept up this speed, then twelve.

Every stump and shard and ridge that lay between himself and the dog he loved, from the tiptop of his head to his toes, looked to Stanley sinister and malevolent. Any hole or ditch might hide a gun. Soldier was almost at the canal. The water would be thick and choked with mud. There he was, out now, on this side of the canal. He had to cross the plain now, cross it from Stanley's ten o'clock. With gathering speed, Soldier soared over something, perhaps a dyke, perhaps a runnel, and Stanley felt a vaulting rush of joy. The pulse of his own heart was suspended, keeping pace with the unending, coalescing step of those quicksilver legs. All his breath converged on that one body—it was only the silver streak that he saw. With pride and hope he watched the gathering speed, the coiled back, the outstretched neck, the outstretched tail. He saw the smooth liquidity and grace of a dog who raced with every atom of his being toward the boy he loved.

The going was heavier now, the mud thick and greedy; Soldier's butterfly legs would be sinking in the evil, foul-smelling slime, but there around his neck, in the tin cylinder, was the precious message, the message that might save Tom.

Like quicksilver Soldier ran on. Around him lay scattered the bodies of the dead. There'd been no time to clear the dead, to collect the wounded. Stanley watched, Hamish watched—James, Fidget, Cook, the line of Australians, a row of hats cresting the parapet for as far as the eye could see, all watching as Soldier hurled himself into the glimmering disc of a shell hole, hitting it at full speed, with a rainbow shower of droplets. He was out—back in the open—would now climb the exposed bank.

There was a stutter of machine-gun fire.

Hamish's hand rose in horror to his face. He shook his head. "A light Maxim. Four hundred rounds."

But Soldier was running onward, unflinching, open-jawed, grinning. He'd been out of range. There was silence from the deadly Maxim. Stanley pictured the evil rounds on their fabric belt, feeding into that gun, knew that its range was four thousand yards. Where was the Maxim? Was Soldier coming into or going beyond the gunner's range?

"There's one gunner—only one on the Maxim," whispered Hamish, adding, "Run, doggie. Run, while he reloads."

In which chink of this malevolent swamp was the Maxim hidden? The machine gun gave a second savage cackle of fire. The gunner had sharpened his aim. Bullets, the size of marbles, fell like hail, whipping and tearing up the ground around Soldier. Was the Maxim on the railway line?

"Come on . . . Come on . . . Hurry, Soldier, hurry . . ."

Stanley could think of nothing, hear nothing, see nothing, only that mercury thread, only the grey form that skimmed the ground like a rushing shadow. A trench festooned with barbed wire lay ahead. Soldier raced toward it and hurdled, joyous, and effortless as a stag, hind legs tucked up. It would be harder going now, the ground a soupy morass—a porridge Hamish called it—but the dusk was deepening and Soldier could use the runnels for cover if they weren't full of water.

There was a single crack of fire from the right—not the Maxim, a rifle.

"A Mauser, there, right below," said Hamish. "Enemy outposts everywhere."

Stanley's head swung wildly—where, where was the gun, where was Soldier?

At the bottom of the slope to Stanley's right, unearthly shades of grey and green and brown mingled.

"Jerry's all around and everywhere," said Fidget.

Still Soldier ran on unhurt and Stanley breathed again.

The line of hats cresting the parapet were all watching, screaming, shouting, and cheering the dog on.

There were two, perhaps three rifle shots. Where was he?
Soldier had disappeared—No, he'd dropped into the dyke,
the flooded dyke, which ran perpendicular to the trench at
the bottom of the slope. He was taking cover—No, he was
out—forced out by the choking mud, perhaps—back out into
the open.

There was not an ounce of cover now. Only the shards of
things that had once been. Only them and this valiant grey
dog. Beyond Soldier, the smoldering village was silhouetted
against an ever-changing backdrop of light. The sky, scintil-
lating over the village, was hung with ribbons of light.

The rifle gave a single brutal crack. Stanley's blood ran
cold. Where was he? Where was Soldier?

"He's up, laddie—he's up," said Hamish.

There . . . There! He'd fallen but he was up on his feet
again the instant he'd landed—it was just the impact that had
thrown him, that was all, just the impact. Stanley's fist was in
his mouth.

Soldier stopped and uttered an unearthly, spine-chilling
shriek of pain. Soldier had been hit. He'd stopped. His
right flank was shuddering, crumpling. Stanley heard, as
though blurred, the screams of the men who watched over
the parapet, saw Hamish's large hands fly to cover a face that
was harrowed with pain, saw him turn aside from a sight
that was beyond bearing. He saw as if at second hand, or in
a dream, Soldier fall . . .

"Soldier, Soldier," he breathed.

He took up his glasses, scanning the waste of slime, his

hands shaking, legs buckling beneath him, his field of vision jumping from one point to another. He saw torn cloths that fluttered in the wind and dead men lying like wreckage brought in on a tide. Where? Where was Soldier? Stanley saw tangled wire, tins, weapons. He saw the dead and the wounded—but where was Soldier?

"Soldier . . ." he breathed, seeing there, on the shining slime, the dog lying like a rag doll, broken limbs sprawling. Stanley turned away, gripping the wooden post, but Hamish was pulling him, turning him back to face the Front.

"Look, laddie, look."

Soldier had raised his head. He was up, up on three legs, forelegs shaking, the slender jaws open and panting, one hind leg trailing. What Stanley couldn't see with his eyes he could feel in his heart—the pain and fear and the reproach with which those eyes would surely be filled.

Soldier was moving forward, pulled still, despite the trailing limb, by the mysterious magnetic tug to his master. On he limped up the slope, tentative as he balanced on his shattered leg.

"Come, boy, come." The closer Soldier drew, the farther out of range he'd be. Only a hundred yards or so up the steepest incline and he'd be safe.

Stanley was trembling from top to toe with fear for Soldier, shivering too in his sodden, unwieldy coat. He yanked the Queen Anne's lace aside, getting a sharp burst of its rank stench.

"Keep going, laddie, keep going," whispered Hamish.

There was another whip crack from the Mauser, then another. Mud spurts burst up. Stanley gripped Hamish's hand—bullets whipped the ground around Soldier, sending up spurts of mud and earth in a radius around the dog. Where was the sniper? Stanley scrabbled at the slithering, crumbling walls of the trench, trying to get higher, to see better. Where was the sniper with the deadly aim, the sniper with the deadly Mauser?

"Five rounds—he's fired five. He's reloading. Keep moving, doggie, keep moving. Keep moving while he reloads."

On he came, valiant forelegs sinking and sliding at every step, the uneven uphill gallop beyond bearing. Stanley's own left hand was on his hip, pressing as though to subdue the pain of a shattered leg. On either side men were screaming for Soldier. Grown men, the same men who'd with dry eyes watched their companions die—these men who'd been so long from women or children or any kind of tenderness—were brought to tears by a dog trailing his broken leg through a storm of fire.

"Keep moving, keep moving . . ." Stanley's eyes were blurred with tears, his fists clenched in a prayer. "Soldier, Soldier . . ."

The Mauser cracked into fire—one—two—three—Soldier's step faltered—four—five—His right flank was quivering now like the surface of a stream—He fell.

Soldier's slender forelegs were aligned to his course, the tortured, twisted right haunch hideous and askew as though wrenched from its socket. Both haunches had now been hit, right and left.

"Oh, laddie!" Both Hamish and James were ashen, devastated, beaten, all hopes of receiving word from the men in the wood now lost.

Seconds passed. An unending, breath-held eternity. The men who had been screaming were silent, their faces constricted. Stanley watched Soldier's head, praying for even the flicker of an ear. Beyond Soldier, amid the darker tangle of wire and weapons, a torn cloth fluttered in the wind, like a hand waving, but the slate-grey body, the pole star of Stanley's hope, lay still. The shiny slime caught the slanting sun in a halo around the motionless form. Nothing else on earth existed for Stanley, only that twisted, fallen body.

"Call him, Stanley, call him," said Fidget. Stanley shot around to Fidget—had he seen the dog move? But Stanley couldn't call until he'd rid his throat of the stone that was lodged there. He tried.

"Soldier!"

There was no movement.

"Louder, Stanley, call louder," urged Fidget.

"Soldier!" Stanley's voice rang out like a bell.

Soldier's ears pricked, his snout lifted perhaps an inch above the ground and his head turned like a heliotrope toward his master's voice.

"Call, laddie, call again," urged Hamish.

Stanley lifted his head above the parapet. He scrambled for footholds in the slithery, cascading wall, and again he called. Soldier rose on his forelegs, jaws open and panting. He took a gallant double leap forward, but he was mired by the dead weight of his useless hindquarters, couldn't heave his rump onward. Stanley watched, agonized, the heartbreaking gallantry, the forelegs shaking with strain as again they pounced forward, but still his rump didn't shift. He pawed the ground with a defiant tilt to his head, pawed it again as though the steep slope itself perhaps had to answer for all this, then he lifted his head and barked and stretched out and again jumped his forelegs onward as though to split himself in two, all his longing to reach his master expressed in his extended neck and shaking legs.

Stanley put a fist in his mouth to stop the scream of pain that was rising inside him.

Soldier pawed the ground.

Seconds passed. Soldier's head and chest sank to the ground.

"It's too much, aye, too much. Half his body weight . . ." said James.

The Company of Signals staff huddled around Stanley began to look away, their faces haunted.

Hamish put an arm around Stanley and dipped his head, turning the boy away from the parapet.

Minutes passed. The first star was lit. The silver discs of craters began to spangle the ground like sequins. On each disc rose a blood-red moon, a thousand crimson globes on a thousand silver seas.

"Up on my shoulders. Let him see you," said Hamish, and he and James laced their fingers as though helping a toddler to mount a pony.

Stanley balanced on the four large McManus hands and pulled himself up. He wasn't high enough, Soldier wouldn't see him; he must stand clear of the parapet, stand on the ridge. Stanley jumped up, the squelching, sucking sound of the mud beneath his boots enough to wake the Kaiser's whole army.

"No, laddie, no! Down—the sniper."

Stanley stood on the ridge, all fear for himself lost in fear for Soldier, and called, "Soldier!" and again, "Soldier!" Standing tall and exposed, the slope and the plain laid out below him, he called one last desperate time, "Soldier!"

There was no movement. He must whistle. If there were breath in Soldier, he'd remember that whistle and lift his head. Stanley fumbled in his pocket, found the box, pushed it open with clumsy, shaking fingers, put the reed to his mouth, and blew.

The luminous notes danced in a bright stream over the desolate plain. A single ear flickered and turned. Stanley blew again. Both ears pricked. Stanley blew once more. Soldier lifted his head, rose on his forelegs; his chest and head were up and he was pawing the ground.

"Soldier!" Stanley called.

There was the smack of a rifle shot and a hammer-blow to his arm. He clenched it below the elbow, half conscious of the seeping wetness, the ferrous smell of blood where the bullet had grazed his arm.

"Get down, laddie!" Hamish cried out.

Still standing, swaying a little, Stanley let go his arm, raised his whistle once more and blew. Soldier moved one foreleg. Then the other. He'd inched forward, he'd dragged his rump on. The right foreleg, quivering with strain, moved again, then the left.

Time expelled everything but the dog from its orbit, and slowed to a standstill, as Stanley watched Soldier fight beyond the limits of endurance, of duty, and of love.

Stanley crouched. Step by step the valiant, trembling

forelegs hauled the mutilated rump over the mutilated ground, inch by dreadful inch, till Stanley could bear no more and threw himself to the ground.

Using his good arm, nose to the brackish, vile-smelling mud, he dragged himself across the flat ground in front of the parapet and down. Inch by inch, seeping scarlet into the shining slime, boy and dog clawed their way toward each other.

There were only yards between them now. Stanley was trembling uncontrollably, each deafening squelch rattling his nerves. His hand clenched a torn bit of clothing, a sleeve perhaps, that made him start as though he'd seen a ghost. Stanley reached forward and with one last desperate stretch he had Soldier's head in his hands, was pulling him close.

Soldier wrenched free. With the last of his strength he rose, his forelegs slithering as he tried to sit, lift his chest, raise his head to his master. The slender jaws were open and grinning, his eyes brilliant. Senseless with pain and love, Stanley could not move to retrieve the message. Soldier raised his snout a little higher. Still the boy made no move. Soldier pawed the ground, his tail flipping. Stanley's gut convulsed, his words strangled and choked.

"Good boy, good . . ."

He snapped the cylinder off the collar with a sharp twist. "Down, boy, down. Lie." Stanley turned to the row of slouch hats cresting the parapet. He raised his good arm and hurled the cylinder over, saw Hamish catch it, then turned and slipped a soggy biscuit fragment into Soldier's jaws.

Early evening, 24 April 1918

Aquenne Wood

Cursing the pain that seared his arm, he eased his coat off and spread it out. Gently he inched it under Soldier, pulled the dog and coat under him, knotting the sleeves behind his back. Carrying the dog in a hammock beneath him, Stanley crawled toward a shallow runnel that lay a few feet away.

"Adjust your sights to the hollow tree trunk to the forward right," he heard someone yell to the gunners. Stanley crawled on. Soldier's message would have identified the hollow trunk that hid the sniper with the deadly aim. Cradling the wounded dog, Stanley edged into the runnel.

"Blast it. Give it all you've got," came the instruction to the gunners.

Five minutes passed. When the firing stopped and Stanley looked out, not a shard remained standing.

"Adjust your sights. Two o'clock. The eastern edge of the Monument. Give it all you've got."

Stanley heard again the pounding of his own artillery.

"For you, Tom," he said. "For you."

The runnel was perhaps three feet deep, just enough to shelter a boy and a dog. They lay side by side, Stanley combing Soldier's mud-choked coat inch by inch with his fingers. Soldier's arteries hadn't been hit, the bleeding was only superficial. There was a bullet wound on the left flank, a round, deep puncture. On the right hind leg another three in a cluster. They must wait here, mustn't risk moving Soldier till they were rescued.

Stanley rested his head next to Soldier's, feeling his warm breath, watching as linesmen crawled forward over the slime making hurried repairs. Stanley saw fresh troops saunter up in endless ranks with a confident swagger, not through the communication trench, but over the top—Australians—their slouch hats silhouetted in the moonlight.

The moon rose higher, a full, red moon. When would he and Soldier be rescued? A wounded dog would be a low priority, Stanley's own wound a low priority. The counterattack would go ahead, but still the wounded and the dead would be left where they lay.

"Open up. Open up. Open up." Brigadier-General Glasgow rose and stood, clear against the night sky. "There's no time for reconnaissance and you don't know the ground but you'll surprise an exhausted enemy. Don't stop till you've taken the Monument, then hold on, at all costs."

As far as Stanley could see in either direction, a single file of men rose from the moon-silvered ridges and crests of trenches.

"Go forward, kill every bloody German that you see. Goodbye, boys—it's neck or nothing."

Stanley watched the Australians saunter off, rifles cocked, as casual as if going after rabbits. A Company detached itself from the main body. It drew up in absolute silence and halted level with the runnel. Every head turned. In perfect formation, they raised their rifles.

"To you, soldier dog," they shouted as one. "To you, soldier boy." As one, each fired a single shot to the sky, lowered their rifles and, again, in perfect formation and with dazzling gallantry, began a jog down the stiff slope to join the main advance.

In an instant a hundred enemy flares shot up like Roman candles, making the plain as light as day. The Australians, roaring and running now like a Viking horde, plunged toward the Monument and the burning buildings of the village. More German SOS shells rose. Leaving fantastic firework trails, they arced and stayed suspended before bursting into a brilliant light and floating dreamily to the ground.

Stanley's arm was burning hot, yet he was shivering. Soldier was scratching one forepaw with the other, scraping them on the ground. He must feed Soldier more of Fidget's biscuit. He fumbled in his pockets but Soldier was too distracted, his frantic paws scrabbling and scratching at the earth bank.

Gas! Gas had poisoned the mud between his pads, was burning him like acid. In the brilliant white light of a flare, Stanley saw Soldier's eyes, gooey and gummed together. He put his head to Soldier's chest and heard the hissing, crackling breath. The water and the thick, stale air of the runnel were poisoned. Stanley gulped the damp night air but his head was too heavy, there were stones in his chest. The ditches and dykes and the shell holes, they were all deadly.

How long would it be before someone rescued them?

Crazy flashes slashed the plain. The wild onslaught ran

onward. The town flared up under a shell like an evil pyre, making of the moon a ball of fire, of the plain a field of blood, bathing the slope in ghastly crimson.

Stanley's aching fingers released their grip on the crumbling bank. His bad arm was throbbing and pulsing from shoulder to fingertip. He was shivery, with fits of hot and cold, so tired he neither knew nor cared where he was. The ground was falling away beneath him. They might be buried alive, he and Soldier, while Amiens was saved, while Paris was saved.

There was a new, stabbing pain in Stanley's chest, knives in his throat. Why were the sky and the earth darker than before? Was it the darkness that was burning his eyes, blistering his throat? If only he could pull down the woolly sky, wrench fistfuls of it over him to muffle the groans and wails of wounded men, the faint despairing moans that pierced the night. He must let his streaming eyes close. Sleep, sleep would ease his pain.

Stanley drifted in and out of wakefulness.

He was forced out of sleep by violent choking. Did someone have a hand down his throat? Stanley's empty body convulsed and he retched until there was nothing left inside except darkness and needles. Now there was poisoned water too, rising, flooding his chest, forcing its way up, brackish and vile into his throat, his mouth. Darkness and needles and poisoned water filled the burning space behind his eyes and pressed him into oblivion.

Before Dawn, 25 April 1918

Aquenne Wood

Cool fingers held Stanley's wrist, then rested on his forehead.

"Half dead. No more 'n a child."

Stanley tilted his face toward the voice and tried to open his gluey eyes. His right arm jerked to his eyes and rubbed them.

"Don't touch or you'll make them worse."

Stanley's arm was restrained and moved to his side.

"These drops will dim your sight till you can see nothing, and that will be a blessing to you."

Amid the fog of pain and nausea, there were paws scrabbling at his shirt, quick panting animal breath on his face.

"Orderly! Over here! Get the dog off him."

Stanley's chest tightened with panic.

"Off. Off!"

Soldier's paws tore at his chest but Stanley's arms were pinned down, his head raised, a bandage wrapped around his eyes. He must hold Soldier, keep him close, but he couldn't move his own head, his arms, couldn't make them do his bidding. His clothes were on fire, searing him.

"I said, get that animal off him."

There was a snarl as the tremulous body on Stanley's chest was wrenched away.

"Get the dog off."

Where were they taking Soldier? Stanley had to summon some strength, had to tell the man that he couldn't take Soldier away, but his clothes were searing his skin, burning thorns were pricking his raw flesh. He swayed and fell back.

"Here you—stretcher-bearer!" another voice shouted.

Someone was cleaning the wound on Stanley's arm. Now he was being hauled up but his legs were buckling beneath him. Stanley's good arm was hooked around someone's shoulder, a sling was hooped around his neck, and his bad arm eased in. Stanley must fight the needles in his throat, must ask the man holding him—Soldier, where was Soldier?

"You can count yourself lucky you can't see what I can see. There's bits and pieces of men all over and nothing we can do for 'em . . ."

One single thought filled Stanley's entire being, one longing: he must commandeer his useless limbs, must ask, "My dog? Where's my dog?"

He'd made only a feeble gurgling sound, must lift his head, and try again.

"Soldier!" But he made no sound and his chest was racked with screaming, throbbing pain.

"He wants the dog."

"Well, I'm not carrying every dead quadruped out of this swamp—there's tops and tails of 'em all over and these are Medical Corps, not veterinary stretchers."

"Keep moving."

Stanley felt the sharp prick of what might be a bayonet.

"Move on. Hop it." There was the click of a rifle loading.

"I'll keep the tip of this little toothpick to your backside to speed you along. Now hop it. We're taking you to the Casualty Clearing Station."

Stanley was forced forward, crumpling into the arms which held him, legs buckling beneath him, head straining to where he thought Soldier might have been.

Stanley's good arm rested on the shoulder of the man in front, his left on the handle of a crutch, another man's hand on his own shoulder. They'd come out of the trenches, there were no duckboards beneath his feet, just cobbles. Around him, men whimpered and moaned. There was something over his shoulders, a blanket perhaps, pressing on his burning skin. His lungs tore at every breath. His bandaged eyes were weeping and clogged. Darkness pressed against his eyes, filling his head, suffocating him. The line shuffled forward, and gentle hands pushed Stanley on, his legs moving without any volition of his own, each buckling step taking him farther from Soldier. If only he could let go, sink down, numb to fear and pain and grief.

Somewhere to Stanley's left there was a shout and a clattering, the rattling of iron on stone, the snorting and whinnying of a horse. Stanley smelt dung and sweat and the thick breath of horses. There were pounding hoofs, a startled whinny, a horse out of control.

"Squadron Leader Ryder, sir!" a young voice called out. There was another frightened whinny.

Stanley's heart vaulted, throttled guttering noises came

from his mouth. Tom! That would be Tom. Stanley must get to him, must get the bandage off his eyes. Dropping his crutch, he tore at the blindfold with his good arm—where was that voice? He must stop his legs from bending, must get to Tom.

There were running footsteps again to Stanley's left. He reached out, but his hand caught only empty air and the footsteps ran on past.

"Squadron Leader Ryder!" that first voice cried out, and there was another whinny. Stanley felt a light hand on his shoulder, pushing him forward. Another voice drifted to him through the thick sea of fever.

"Fifty light draft horses, sir, and twenty draft mules, all properly branded and shod, sir."

Stanley stopped and swung his head toward that voice. The man behind him shuffled forward, caught the back of Stanley's right boot and Stanley fell. Lying doubled up with pain, he called out, "Tom!"

Gentle hands raised him to his feet. Stanley shook himself free.

"Tom! Tom!" Stanley's throat was tearing; he'd called out but his words had been no more than a strangled, guttering sound. His right hand scrabbled in his pocket. With shaky fingers, he pushed open the matchbox, pulled out the whistle, and blew. Notes, too faint for anyone to hear but him, dissolved before they'd risen. He had no breath, there were knives in his throat, no breath in his constricted, gurgling chest.

Stanley must try one last time. Again he blew and the notes were clean and bright but officious hands took his shoulders, pulled him back, pushed him on.

The line shuffled forward, then paused and Stanley waited, head hanging.

Somewhere someone was running, now stopping, now running again. Every muscle tense, amid the sounds of wheels and hoofs and shuffling boots, Stanley strained to hear those running feet. Nothing. They'd stopped—but there was a new sound—powerful, rippling notes that soared and bubbled in a bright fountain. A whistle—a reed whistle—the notes of the moors, of sunlit uplands and drystone walls, the sound of his boyhood. Stanley's heart vaulted. His urgent, shaking hand, fumbled for his whistle. Needles jabbed his throat, but with the last of his strength and the last of his breath, he blew. Clear strong notes were rising, floating upward. A trembling second passed, then someone was running, stopping, running again. Stanley stretched his arm out, blind, in the empty air, turning and turning in the darkness. His hand was taken, lowered to his side and he was turned, wrapped in strong arms, was dissolving against a broad chest, feeling the damp on his da's cheeks, Da's hand stroking his own head.

"Son . . ."

Stanley's right arm rose, his fingers clawed at the bandages on his eyes; he wanted to see Da's face.

"Squadron Leader Ryder! At the double!"

"He's here, son, your dog is here. I'm here to find him, to find him, to return him to you."

Stanley nodded and made a choking sound. Da put his forehead to Stanley's and they stayed there a second, temple to temple.

"Messenger Dog 2176. They told me he's here."

An immense sob rose within Stanley's chest and he raised his bandaged eyes, nodding urgently in the direction from which he thought he'd come. He heard Da's sharp intake of breath.

"What happened, son? Where is he?"

If Stanley talked with his mouth only, not his throat, perhaps he could just form the words with his lips.

"I couldn't see him, Da." Stanley's voice was a desperate whisper but he wasn't stuttering, his words were forming as he wanted them to. "They took me away . . . left him out there." He could feel Da's breath against his face, then felt Da's lips on his forehead. He clawed again at the bandages on his eyes; he had to see Da—the bandage was in his mouth but his hand caught air as he tried to touch Da.

"I can't see you, Da."

"Squadron Leader Ryder! At the double!"

Da lifted the bandage and put it back over Stanley's eyes. He took Stanley's hands in his own, touching his temple again to Stanley's, then turning him forward.

"Go on, Stanley, go on to the hospital. I'm to take the horses up to the Front for the Artillery. Go on, son, and I'll come for you as soon as I come down the line."

Guided on by orderlies, the line shuffled forward into a hushed, tented area. There were whispering, bustling voices. A nurse was snipping through Stanley's uniform, unwinding his field dressing, cleaning his wound.

"Pre-op tent," she said. Stanley's boots were unlaced and he was lowered on to a bed.

His pain unraveled, and he slid away.

27 April 1918

Casualty Clearing Station, Crouay

Everything was quiet. The men around Stanley were sleeping. He'd been moved to an evacuation tent. He knew he had a sign above his bed, that it said "GAS CASE, MODERATE." Pain pounded the front of his head. His every breath was quick and forced, every cough a knife wound. Nurse said his eyelids were swollen and sticky, the eyelashes burned away. Nurse's voice was always tired and sad. She said they had beds for three hundred and fifty men, but there were thousands here, more wounded streaming in, that in corridors, in the spaces between beds, men lay unattended, dying.

How long had Stanley been here? He must go and find Soldier. Soldier would be hungry now, his wounds must be treated. Stanley mustn't be evacuated, not till he'd found Soldier. When Nurse came around Stanley would ask for help but now he was too drugged, his limbs drowsy and leaden. He must let himself drift away.

"Now, keep still. I'll put some drops in your eyes. There, keep still."

Twice a day the goggles on his eyes were removed.

"Well done, now the other one. It's been three days now and your arm's healing ever so well. Today we'll take the goggles off for good, put bandages on instead, and we'll hope for the best."

When Nurse came around again, she put him in fresh flannelette pajamas. She gave him a bowl of milk and rice and told him that his lungs would recover, but said nothing about his eyes. Stanley didn't want milk and rice. He wasn't hungry unless it was for soft toast and honey, but the pajamas felt cool against his burning skin.

"Stay with me a little," he whispered. They were the first words he'd spoken since arriving here but he hadn't tripped over them, they'd come out as he wanted them to. "Will you take my bandages off?" Nurse was silent. "My dog is out there, Nurse. Dog number 2176. I must go and get him. Will you take the bandages off my eyes?"

Nurse didn't answer, but she sat by Stanley for a while in silence, holding his hand in hers.

"When will you take away the bandages so that I can see?"

Still Nurse didn't answer. After a while she kissed his forehead and Stanley felt what may or may not have been a tear falling beside the kiss.

In the morning the Medical Orderly told Stanley that he was quite blind, that there was only a small chance of his eyes recovering.

"How small?" Stanley's voice wobbled and frayed like a child's. He didn't hear the orderly's answer, if there was one.

Outside shells were falling somewhere. Were they falling where Tom was? Where Soldier was? Where Da was? It was, thought Stanley, after all, easier not to see in such a world. He lay awake dreading the night which came and gave him back his day, for when he slept, he'd dream as though he had his sight again and he'd see only what he'd already seen, the breakneck run, the torn and sprawling limbs.

Nurse came and stood by him and put a good, cold sponge on his forehead. She told Stanley she was changing the sign above his bed, that it said "ENGLAND," that he'd be going home, and she sounded pleased for him.

"Did they find him? Did they bring my dog back?"

Stanley felt the cold sponge on his forehead again, but heard no answer.

"Dog number 2176. I have to find my dog—"

"There, there . . . You'll feel better in the morning."

Home meant nothing without Soldier, without Da, without Tom. Stanley couldn't leave France without Soldier. He'd come so far, but had caused nothing but harm. He'd led his own innocent dog into an inferno, his own elderly father into a world of senseless death.

On the third day his bandages were removed and replaced with a thin layer of gauze. Stanley opened his eyes. He saw shapes and shadows but he thought only of Soldier, of Da, of Tom. The wound on his arm was healing but he must try to keep it still. That afternoon, still as weak and blind as a newborn puppy, Stanley was moved, by hospital train, farther from the Front, from Soldier, to the General Hospital at Etaples.

On her night-time round, a nurse called Queenie washed Stanley's eyes and applied ointment.

"There's a brand new moon out there, just there, in the window above your head. You must turn your money and wish. Wish, Stanley, that you're lucky and your eyes keep getting better."

She went on down the ward, with a hopeful thought for each man. She reached the door and paused. Stanley could see movement—she'd be buttoning her coat perhaps? Queenie called out a cheery goodnight. There was another movement somewhere along the row of beds, between the door and Stanley. Someone was standing up on his bed, had begun to sing in a good baritone.

"Come on now—altogether, boys."

The whole ward joined in an enthusiastic chorus. Queenie helped her troubadour from his bed and—were they dancing? Stanley heard the soft patter of his bare feet, her shoes, on the boards, saw her dark coat, his pale pajamas—they were! They were dancing, twirling up and down between the beds, as lightly as though they'd never seen a war. Stanley would never be able to do that, would never dance like that, with so light a heart.

The next night there was a concert. There was lemonade, biscuits, sweets, cigarettes. Queenie sat beside Stanley on an upturned crate. Catcalls, whistles, and applause greeted each act. Stanley's left arm was still bandaged so Queenie joined her left hand to Stanley's right to make two to clap with. A group of men came on stage. Stanley could see them, see the shapes of them—it was true what Queenie said, that his eyes were getting better.

When the audience was finally silent, the men on stage began to sing, "Hush, here comes a whizz-bang . . ."

There was a pause, an expectant silence. Then the ear-piercing screech of an approaching shell, growing louder, mad confusion as men dived for cover under chairs, tables, crates. The screech curved away and died without an explosion. There was a loud, stagey whisper: "Where did that one go to, 'Erbert?"

Roaring with laughter, men crawled out, laughing at their own fear, laughing that they'd been so fooled by a recording.

Alone amid the clattering of chairs and the relieved laughter, Stanley was numb with fear, glued to his chair, his knuckles white where they gripped his knees. He saw Soldier's joyous, weightless gallop, his laughing jaws and narrowed, smiling eyes. He saw too a spume of earth erupting and the shattered, sprawling limbs.

Jagged convulsions rattled Stanley's body. He whimpered helplessly. Queenie wrapped him in his blanket and led him from the room.

PART III

8 June 1918

St. Dunstan's Hostel for the Blinded, Regent's Park, London

Stanley smelt fresh-cut grass. He heard breeze in the rustling acacia and he heard birdsong, but the birdsong and the breeze were muffled and dislocated, like distant memories from far beyond or below the din of a war, which screeched still in his ears.

There was a burst of laughter from the hazy group playing dominoes under the mulberry tree. Stanley shrank away, pulling the blanket tighter around him. He could see well enough now, Matron had said that his eyes would make a full recovery, but Stanley knew, too, that his sight would be forever haunted by the slender, silver head of the dog he'd loved, the dog he'd left to die in a poisoned runnel. No, Da hadn't drowned Soldier: in the end it had been he himself who'd taken the dog to his death. When he'd run away from home, how little he'd thought that he'd turn his world inside out, that it would all end like this, himself in England, Da in France.

Stanley's shoulders slumped and he withdrew into his chair. Yes, he thought, yes, this is how Da had used to sit, hunched in his red chair, unseeing and far beyond the world. Stanley had so misunderstood the depth of Da's fear and grief that he'd accused him of a terrible cruelty, of a crime he'd never committed. Yes, he thought, remembering Da's letter. Yes, Da, a full circle has been turned. I understand now. Your heart was so wrung by Ma's death that you locked it up.

Stanley shuddered and covered his eyes with his hands. He couldn't turn back the clock and new understanding couldn't give him ease or release. Still the memories of Bones, of Soldier, of Da, burned like boiling water on open wounds. Stanley pummeled his forehead with his fists.

Shouts of friendly competition from the rowers on the lake shimmered up to the satin sky. The cheerful whistling of the cobblers eddied up from the township of huts below the lawn. Stanley heard the cries of the rowers, and in them heard manliness and hope, and he dipped his head in shame. The soldiers here liked to row and to dance, to go out on to the lawn with their blankets and their dominoes; they were happy to be alive, they were grateful, and they were all quite blind. They had been carried over the dead point and faced their futures with courage and hope. Stanley had no courage left, no hope, had remained washed up at the dead point. As Da had been when Ma died.

Only Stanley, in this creamy Regency Villa, would recover his sight fully. When he looked in the mirror, he could see that his cornea were bright and clear, but his eyes were older, beyond tears, beyond laughter, an old man's eyes in a young man's face. He'd been lucky, very lucky, so Matron said. She kept saying, too, that his was a joyous case, that he'd regained his sight almost entirely. But she'd say that with her troubled voice and he knew he shouldn't still be here, that perhaps they needed his bed for another man, that Matron didn't know what to do with him, that the Adjutant didn't know what to do with him, that the Commandant didn't know what to do with him.

Tom.

This morning he'd been so sure he might hear from him. If Tom were alive, there'd be a letter from him. On this day of all days, there'd have been a letter. Fifteen today. Tom wouldn't forget, had never forgotten his brother's birthday before. But when they'd all filed along the linoleum path after breakfast, toward the terrace room, with its smell of beeswax and fresh-cut flowers, the Voluntary Aid Detachment nurse (VAD), with her white cap and apron with the red cross on the bib, had had armfuls of post, but nothing for Stanley.

A card from Lara had arrived yesterday. She'd asked after his eyes, said how lucky he was, and hoped he'd be home soon. She hadn't mentioned Tom or Da and Stanley had let the card drop, didn't know where it was now. Joe had sent Stanley another pack of playing cards and a note saying that he was on a winning streak, was looking forward to playing with Stanley again, longing to hear all he had to tell. Father Bill had written too, to say he was glad Stanley was back in England, to wish him a full recovery, but he'd made no mention of Da or Tom.

Then when the VAD had read aloud from the *Illustrated News*, there'd been an item on Kemmel and she'd read of scenes of appalling horror, of five thousand unidentifiable French dead, of six thousand captured. The numbers of British dead had not been mentioned. If Tom had survived

Villers, would he have had orders for Kemmel? Would Da have been at Kemmel? James and Hamish—where were they? And Fidget?

The huge clock projecting over the terrace rang out. The two life-sized carved figures bobbed their heads and clubbed their bells. Once, twice, three times. At half past three it would be Visitors' Hour. The hour Stanley most dreaded, the hour of most cheerfulness, the hour of most laughter.

"Happy birthday to you . . ."

Stanley opened his eyes and there, in the dappled light, were Matron's white stockings and black boots. Matron was nice, but she wasn't Tom and she wasn't Da. Stanley summoned a forced, watery smile. Matron's outstretched arms bore a cake. Behind Matron was a trail of men in single file. From the scattered chairs and tables, the other men with useless eyes left their games and gathered around, guided by their VADs.

"Happy birthday to you . . . Happy birthday, dear Stan-ley . . ."

Stanley didn't feel fifteen. He was an old man, an empty vessel, but still he must smile, still he must be grateful.

". . . Happy birthday to you!"

He leaned forward and blew.

Out of the fifteen, three quivering flames to go. He must blow again. Matron handed Stanley a knife.

"Cut a slice, and make a wish." He looked her in the eyes. She knew his wishes needed angels and archangels, cathedrals and choirs, not fifteen candles and a jam sponge.

Matron sliced the cake, chatting all the while. She was

228

used to talking to Stanley and getting no answer. He liked her for not expecting answers, nor forcing them. Matron rose and bustled about with napkins and forks. She stopped by Jim who had no arms. Matron broke off bits of his cake and fed them to him.

Jim grinned. "Mmm. Chocolate cake."

"No, Jim, it's a nice sponge cake, with nice jam in the middle and nice butter icing on the top."

Jim would never see again but he could still smile and enjoy sponge cake. Stanley could see, knew that he'd been lucky, but he could not feel, could not care.

Matron returned to Stanley and picked up the Veterinary Science book beside Stanley's chair. "I hope you're not straining your eyes—only two hours a day . . . it's very small print."

Stanley heard in her voice that sort of troubled tone she seemed to keep just for him. Matron was running her hand back and forth along the book's spine, thinking. Stanley, too, looked at the spine, thinking he must study hard, return to school, be, one day, a vet.

The visitors had begun to arrive, were hurrying down the steps between the roses on to the lawn. The group around Stanley dispersed. Matron drew up a chair.

Had there still been no word about Soldier, about Tom, about Da, from the Secretary's Office?

Matron was looking away toward the French windows. Stanley would speak first, he would ask his questions first; he'd ask her again, hadn't asked since yesterday. He wouldn't ask more than once a day but he longed to know, to be certain about what had happened. If Soldier had been found . . . The AVC who'd seen Bones had said "any dog unfit for service" would be shot . . . Someone must know, the Dog Service must know. The office conducted an enormous correspondence and finding a missing dog wouldn't be a priority. Perhaps not even a possibility. But he had to know.

"Did you hear anything, Matron? Did they trace him? His number was 2176. Did you tell them that?"

Matron's mouth opened and closed. She glanced again toward the terrace. Stanley tugged her hand.

"Has the Secretary still had no news?"

Matron hesitated, then leaned forward, pulling him toward her, her soft bulk enfolding his stiff, unyielding self. Had Soldier been shot? Been left to die in an open grave? Matron kissed the top of his head and stepped back, resting a hand on each of his shoulders.

"Stanley, the living are more important than the dead. You must remember the living. And you must go home to them." Her eyes creased and a dimple formed in each cheek as she smiled a sort of secret smile. Again she glanced toward the door as though at any moment a visitor for Stanley might materialize where one never had before. She hesitated, then turned back, looking awkward and a little lost for words, her hands seeking refuge beneath her apron in the side pockets of her skirt.

"We're going to get you home this week. Your eyes are good now, and your lungs. You've been so lucky, Stanley." Stanley looked away toward the dotted sunlit groups, the loving clusters of sisters and brothers, sons and daughters, mothers and wives visiting the other men. Go home to what? Where were Tom, Da, Soldier?

"Here . . ." Matron pulled her right hand out of her pocket. "This is for you."

"FOR JUNE 8th" was marked in capitals across the top left of a white envelope. That was Tom's writing—and that was an ordinary Post Office stamp—Tom was alive and he was home.

"You have a father and a brother, Stanley, and they love you," Matron said. Stanley tore at the envelope, read in one stumbling, breathless rush:

> Thornley
> 6th June 1918
> Dear Stanley,
> I arrived home today and am so relieved and so happy to know from Lara and from Matron that you are safe, safe in England, that your sight has returned, your lungs healed and that you'll soon be home for good. The joy of knowing that you are safe overtakes every other feeling and shatters all other sorrows. Until my leg heals, I must stay in bed, so Lara and I wait for you here at Thornley and long for your return.

Stanley looked up at Matron, tears in his eyes, his chin and lips wobbling. Tom was home, Tom was safe. Stanley read on, at breakneck speed, breath held. Da? Soldier? What of them?

It feels strange to me, and will to you too, how unchanged all is here, that the buttercup still comes up before the campion, that butterflies still fly.

I believe my Company was saved that day by a dog. I drew a map that marked the position of an enemy machine gun. We'd no ammunition and no wireless and were pinned to the ground like rats in holes, and that whisper of a dog carried my map over the open ground and up the exposed slope. It was a dog of whom I've never seen the like, a dog so fast you'd barely know it was a dog at all, a dog whose courage and sense of duty you'd not always find in a man, a dog who must have loved his master to his last breath.

"Soldier, Soldier . . . he was my dog, Tom . . . the dog I named for you . . ."

And if you hadn't been there, I would almost have wished you were, so you could see the run he did. That was the first time I saw messenger dogs in action, the first time I understood your work. Stanley, they say Villers was the single greatest action of the War — a night time attack, at short notice, over unknown and difficult ground. It put an end to the German hope of Amiens and Paris. That night changed the tide of the War—it was the last of the retreat, the beginning of the end. The dog saved so many lives at Villers that there's been a new order — from now on all infantry battalions have to have a dog with them.

Da is still on commission taking horses up to the front lines.

Da safe. Tom and Da safe.

He's working with hunters, cobs, coach horses, drays, mules from Minnesota, Percherons from America, but, he says, of course, that no horse he's seen can beat the English riding horse with thoroughbred in its veins. Da knows as much as any man about horses, and cares more than any man. It was all for the best, Stanley, in the end, all that happened. Da's grief has passed and he's busy and happy again, proud to be doing the work he's doing.

Tom, Tom! What of Soldier . . . ?

Kemmel was the worst action that I saw.
There was no cover and the trenches
were so shallow we had to lie in them.
Within an hour seven hundred bombs
were dropped on us. I am lucky to be
alive, lucky to have only an injury to my
leg. I am recommended for a medal for
Kemmel, but the best medal of all will be
when you return.
Happy Birthday, Brother. I think,
after all, it will be your best.
Tom.

Stanley read and reread, reveling in pieces of it, agonizing
in others, reading again and again the whole of it; Tom was
alive, he was back and back for good. He and Lara Bird
were both at Thornley. And the campion was up and there'd
be honey on the table.

A hand ruffled Stanley's hair and he felt the callused
skin of a large palm on his cheek. Stanley froze. His eyes
shifted a fraction from the letter. Matron's white stockings
had vanished, in their place stood a pair of shiny boots and
puttees. Slowly at first, all of him trembling uncontrollably,
Tom's letter rattling in his hands, Stanley's gaze rose inch
by inch, now shot upward.

Above the high, weathered forehead, Da's white hair was dappled with luminous spots of sun. Stanley flung aside his blanket and sprang up, scattering a shower of cake crumbs— He'd come—Da had come to find him—He'd come not once but twice—

"Da—"

"Wait, Stanley. Wait." Da's hand was on his shoulder, holding him down. "Close your eyes and hold out your hand."

Feeling like a small child, Stanley clenched his eyes, but not before he'd seen the proud carriage of the once bent back and the warm light in Da's eyes. Like a child again, Stanley held his palm flat and open. Something cold and metallic was dropped on to it. Stanley paused, then his wary palm cupped it, feeling a cylinder, shaky fingers searching for the opening around the belly of it, thumb finding the ring that once attached it to a collar. His eyes flew open.

The cylinder was engraved:

WAR MESSENGER DOG
NO. 2176

"Open it, Stanley."

Stanley pulled the halves apart, took out the message and read in Da's unpracticed hand, "Yours to keep." Da was stooping over a large hamper, untying twine. The lid was forced up and like shaggy rolling surf something unleashed itself, and in a surge of silvery light vaulted on to Stanley. Balancing on the unsteady ground of Stanley's thighs, it furled and unfurled itself, turning and turning, nosing and nuzzling him. Stanley clenched fistfuls of the long rough coat, smelt Soldier's sweet hay smell, smelt the doggishness of him, felt his tongue lick the wet from his own cheeks and the swoosh of a feathery tail.

"They had to tear the two of you apart, the medical men told me," Da said. "When I found him, he was still there, still waiting. He's a great dog. They told me, your McManus brothers—they came looking for me, Stanley, for me to give you this, and they told me what he did that day—what you and he did together."

Stanley looked at his Da. "What happened to them, Da? Are they—?"

"They tell me Fidget was sent home after that first morning at Kemmel—shell shock, not wounded. Hamish and James, they were both at Kemmel, Stanley, and like Tom, they were lucky."

Soldier organized himself to hold his nose toward his master, waggled his haunches, waggled them again, whirred his tail, tossed his head, and opened his jaws to smile.

"I smuggled him over," Da said. "He's been pretending to be a sandbag for that long—on the boat—on the train—in front of Matron. So he'll be wanting to go home now . . . will be that happy to go home and be a dog again . . . for you to be a boy again."

Soldier steadied his forepaws on the narrow arm of the deckchair, joggled his haunches, raised his snout skyward, and hurled a salvo of woofs to the rustling tracery of the acacia. Away, under the mulberry, the visitors looked up and gawped. By the candyfloss roses Matron stood open-mouthed, gulping, her mighty bosom heaving, her throat constricting as though to expel a frog. Stanley ran his hand down the dog's haunches, tracing the firm raised scars. He tilted his head upward, felt sunlight on his temple, and he saw Da turn aside lest anyone should see his tears.

HISTORICAL NOTE

VILLERS-BRETONNEUX

Villers-Bretonneux was not a great battle but it was a decisive one, putting an end to the German plan of taking Paris. The carnage at Villers-Bretonneux continued until the night of 26 April 1918 when the town and its immediate surroundings fell once more into British hands. During that night French troops relieved the British and Australian forces of a position which had cost the lives of around 10,000 men, killed, wounded, and missing.

Villers has the largest of all First World War military cemeteries.

THE BRITISH MESSENGER DOG SERVICE

When hostilities were declared in August 1914, the German army had 6,000 trained dogs while Britain had no official dog cover.

Colonel Edwin Hautenville Richardson had spent fifteen years training dogs. At the outset of war he decided not to re-enlist, but to continue this work. However, when he offered his help to the War Office, a General responded that his own duty "as a commanding officer would be to prohibit, under all circumstances, the use of dogs . . ." For the next two years, the War Office continued to reject Richardson's offers. However, in 1916, he received an unofficial request for dogs from a Colonel Winter. Richardson sent out two Airedales, Wolf and Prince. When all telephone lines had broken and visual signaling was impossible, Prince delivered a message that saved a battalion of the Sherwood Foresters.

Finally, in November 1917, as casualties soared, the War Office summoned Richardson and established the Messenger Dog Service, to be run as a branch of the Signals Service, with Richardson as Commandant of the Training School. Dogs were recruited from the Battersea, Birmingham, Liverpool, and Manchester homes. Then the Home Office ordered police all over the country to send in strays. Finally, an appeal to the public brought an overwhelming response—7,000 dogs came forward at once.

Commanding officers were, at first, sniffy about the dogs, often ignoring them, until instructions from HQ taught them how to use them. A central kennel was formed at Etaples, from where dogs and keepers were posted to Sectional Kennels behind the front lines. From here, the keepers were sent, with three dogs apiece, up to Brigade HQ. The dogs were then led away by infantrymen up to the front line, while their keepers remained at Brigade HQ, watching for their return, ready to deliver the messages they brought to their commanding officer.

The work of every British dog on the Western Front— each run they made, its distance and destination—is recorded in the DGHQ Central Kennels Register of Dogs and Men (GR Army Book 129). Airedales were eventually named the official breed of the British Army, though it was the ordinary half-bred lurcher that stood out as the messenger dog par excellence.

Some of the events of Bones's and Soldier's lives are based on the dog known as Airedale Jack, who came from the Battersea Dogs Home. In 1918 Airedale Jack was sent to France and taken by the Sherwood Foresters to an advance post at the Front. The Germans cut off every line of communication with Headquarters. No runner could have survived the barrage of gunfire. Jack was released, stayed close to the ground, taking advantage of whatever cover there was, but came under heavy bombardment. A piece of shrapnel smashed his jaw. A missile ripped open his coat from shoulder to thigh. Jack staggered on, using craters and trenches for cover. His forepaw was hit and still he dragged himself along the ground, on three legs, for the last few miles. He reached Headquarters, delivered the message and, having saved the battalion, Airedale Jack fell dead.

In early November 1918, it was ordered that all infantry battalions were to be given messenger dogs. After the Armistice, Field Marshal Haig's final dispatch paid tribute to the work of the dogs. In March 1919 the Service was liquidated.

During the course of the Great War, 100,000 dogs served with the warring nations. Of these, 7,000 were killed.

PHOTO GALLERY

Second Divisional Signals Company members with several messenger dogs in Saint-Gratien, France, 1918. (Australian War Memorial P01836.018)

Two messenger dogs with their British Army handler recover from mustard gas that damaged their paws in Nieppe Wood, France, 1918. (Australian War Memorial H09652)

A captured German Army messenger dog remains still as a British soldier removes a message, France, 1918. (Australian War Memorial H09579)

An informal portrait of the captured German messenger dog that was intercepted in the British lines. (Imperial War Museum)

Corporal James Coull stands with his three charges of the No. 3 Messenger Dog Section connected to the 4th Divisional Signal Company. The photo was taken near Villers-Bretonneux.

The dogs from left to right: War Dog 103 Nell, a Cross Setter; 102 Trick, a Collie; 101 Buller (referred to sometimes as Bullet), an Airedale. (Australian War Memorial E02318)

Bounding over a trench, a German messenger dog makes its way to the desired destination. The photo was possibly taken near Sedan on the Western Front, May 1917. Note the soldiers just below the leaping dog to the left. (Imperial War Museum)

AUTHOR'S NOTE

The idea for this novel came from a story on the radio, a true story, which, even when I sat in the blistering heat, heavily pregnant, and in a traffic jam on Park Lane, sent a shiver down my spine. The program was about the animals who'd given their lives during the Great War, and it was broadcast around the time that the memorial to them was erected on Park Lane. Through my car window, I could see the memorial as I listened.

An Airedale named Jack, recruited by the British Army from the Battersea Dogs Home and trained at the War Dog School, was sent out to the Western Front. Jack's battalion came under heavy fire. If the entire battalion was to survive, it needed reinforcements and ammunition, and no human runner would survive the barrage of gunfire in order to get a message out. One Lieutenant Hunter slipped a message into Jack's collar and said, "Good-bye, Jack. Go back, boy. "

Jack ran off, staying close to the ground, and taking advantage of whatever cover there was, running through deep swamp for over half a mile. Under heavy bombardment, he began to get hit by enemy fire. A piece of shrapnel smashed his jaw. The battalion watched as Jack bravely staggered on.

A missile ripped open his black and tan coat from shoulder to thigh, but still he continued, using shell craters and trenches for cover. His forepaw was hit, and he fell. Jack rose, dragged himself along the ground on three legs for the last few miles, persevering inch by inch, until he reached his master and fell dead at his feet, his jaw broken, his leg splintered. Airedale Jack saved his battalion that day, and earned himself a posthumous Victoria Cross, the highest military decoration award for valor in the United Kingdom.

Before the moment I heard this story, I hadn't known that there'd been seven thousand dogs killed in the Great War. Nor had I known that they'd served as sentinels, scouts, sentries, and ambulance and messenger dogs. I heard stories of other animals there on Park Lane, but it was the idea of the messenger dog, of his intelligence, loyalty, and of the sense of duty that could draw him through gunfire and back to his master, that brought tears to my eyes.

SELECT BIBLIOGRAPHY

Allen, Tony, *Animals at War, 1914–1918*, Great War History 7 (Holgate, 1999)

Baker, Peter Shaw, *Animal War Heroes* (A. & C. Black, 1933)

Baynes, E. H., *Animal Heroes of the Great War* (Macmillan, 1925)

Blenkinsop, L. J., and J. W. Rainey, *Veterinary Services*, History of the Great War (HMSO, 1925)

Clabby, Brigadier J., *The History of the Royal Army Veterinary Corps 1919–1961* (J. A. Allen & Co., 1963)

Gray, Ernest A., *Dogs of War* (Hale, 1989)

Hamer, Blythe, *Dogs at War: True Stories of Canine Courage under Fire* (André Deutsch, 2006)

Moore, Major-General Sir John, *Army Veterinary Service in War* (Brown, 1921)

Richardson, Major E. H., *British War Dogs, Their Training and Psychology* (Skeffington, 1920)

———, War, Police and Watch Dogs (1910)

FROM THE ARCHIVE OF THE IMPERIAL WAR MUSEUM, LONDON:

Waley, Major A. C., GHQ Central Kennels, Register of Dogs and Men

Waley, Major A. C., Messenger Dog Service, July 1917–April 1919

War Diary of OC Carrier Pigeon and Messenger Dog Service 1915–1919

GO FISH

SAM ANGUS

What did you want to be when you grew up?
Oh . . . so many things: nun, pilot, society hostess, author, poet, mountaineer, painter, explorer, fashion designer, ballet dancer—depending on what I was reading at the time, probably. Though I can safely say I have never wanted to be an accountant or a soccer player.

When did you realize you wanted to be a writer?
I always knew I would write something, from when I was very, very young. I never knew when or what, though Lampedusa's example of writing only one brilliant and lasting novel featured prominently as an inspiration.

What's your most embarrassing childhood memory?
Being chosen last for the basketball team.

As a young person, who did you look up to most?
It was always people I met in books. I don't remember meeting anyone or being taught by anyone especially inspirational. As far as I could work out, everyone interesting was either dead or fictional.

What was your favorite thing about school?
My friends.

What were your hobbies as a kid? What are your hobbies now?
Reading and photography. I still do photography now with an old, large format 10 x 8 camera, and any kind of recording of almost anything in scrapbooks, video, albums, etc.

What was your first job, and what was your "worst" job?
I lasted only one day as an employee on a newspaper where they said I was the worst journalist they'd ever come across. I have never done another day's work for anyone else since.

What book is on your nightstand now?
A biography of the explorer Gertrude Bell, *Daughter of the Desert*.

Where do you write your books?
In the car, in the raspberry beds, some of it on my cell phone, almost anywhere my kids can't get ahold of me. In ideal circumstances, I am at my desk.

What sparked your imagination for *Soldier Dog*?
I was stuck in a traffic jam on Park Lane in London, very hot, heavily pregnant, and with no hope of getting on time to wherever it was I needed to be when I turned on the radio and heard Jilly Cooper talking about the dogs who had fought for us during the First World War. As I listened, I could see, through my car window, the memorial that had just been erected to all the animals that had given their lives in both wars. I knew then and there that I would one day tell a story about those dogs.

How did you find out about messenger dogs?

I spent years researching in the archives of the Imperial War Museum, going through letters, unpublished documents, and records of the training of the dogs. Later, I found additional material on the Internet, and there is still more every day. Though sadly, most of the men who worked with the dogs were illiterate and left very little in the way of diaries or letters.

Have you always owned dogs?

Yes. We had dogs at home. Our first dog was a rescue dog called Gitana (Gypsy). I then had a dog while I was at Trinity College in Cambridge and had to smuggle him in and out of the dorm in a laundry bag until he was discovered and I was forced to choose between my dog and my university career. Lord Byron, years before, kept a bear at Trinity, but bears were dealt with more leniently than dogs, I think. I have another dog now, amongst several other animals.

What challenges do you face in the writing process, and how do you overcome them?

The Internet is an enormous benefit, as well as a challenge to concentration, the flood of e-mail being a constant assault.

Which of your characters is most like you?

Stanley is very like me. I didn't stammer as a child, but I was painfully shy, and could barely talk to anyone without turning hot and red. I was also almost as isolated as he was, growing up as I did in several countries, moving from one to another, and each time, not knowing anyone or being able to speak the same language.

What makes you laugh out loud?
I laugh very often. Miranda Hart, *Dad's Army*, and the Pink Panther movies all make me laugh almost as much as an evening out with my girlfriends.

What do you do on a rainy day?
Photographs, films, reading, and banagrams with the kids.

What's your idea of fun?
Physical challenge.

What is your favorite word?
Adventure.

What's your favorite song?
"Don't Fence Me In."

Who is your favorite fictional character?
Velvet in *National Velvet*.

What was your favorite book when you were a kid? Do you have a favorite book now?
The Dolphin Crossing, *The Silver Sword*, *I Am David*. Right now, I am enjoying reading Michael Morpurgo's *The Mozart Question*.

What's your favorite TV show or movie?
Oh, so many. The ones that come to mind immediately are *Invictus*, *Gone with the Wind*, *Into the West*, *Mary Poppins*, *Greyfriars Bobby*, and *National Velvet*.

What's the best advice you have ever received about writing?
Write, just write. And read.

What advice do you wish someone had given you when you were younger?
To pay no heed to what anyone else thinks, ever, and always be as true as you can to yourself. The two generally need to go hand in hand.

Do you ever get writer's block? What do you do to get back on track?
I write.

Do you have any strange or funny habits? Did you when you were a kid?
My husband says my nose twitches when I'm really concentrating on my writing. . . .

What do you wish you could do better?
Sing. I should so love to sing well.

What would your readers be most surprised to learn about you?
They'd be very surprised by some of my school reports. . . . Also perhaps, that I was a ski wear designer for many years before writing.

What do you want readers to remember about your books?
The love, loyalty, tenacity, and resilience of my heroes.

War took his hope, a horse gave him courage.

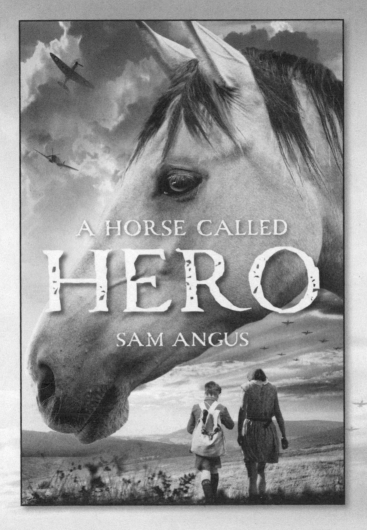

A HORSE CALLED

HERO

SAM ANGUS

Turn the page for a sneak peek of

A HORSE CALLED HERO

Chapter One

Wolfie stopped, distracted by the stacks of sandbags and newly dug trenches. Above Rotten Row, silver barrage balloons strained and sang on their cables. They were like sails in a high wind, he thought, or great prehistoric birds. Tolerant of her small and willful brother, Dodo waited, sighing loudly as Wolfie turned to look at some cavalry, dropping his gas mask to the ground. A team of grey horses was trotting brightly up the South Carriage Drive. Wolfie watched, transfixed; Captain had been a grey too. After the war Pa had ridden Captain along the North Ride for the Victory Parade of 1918, the medal on his chest, the cheering crowds, all captured in Ma's photograph on the mantel at home.

The horses drew closer and halted, luminous and magical as a troop of moons come down to earth. A frown creased Wolfie's brow. He remembered Pa, here in the park, after war broke out, the day before he'd left to fight again in France. He remembered how he'd turned, white-faced, from the animals he so loved, and said, "I hate all of it and what it stands for . . ." Wolfie had felt confused then, and shocked, and still felt confused now.

He gave a determined shrug, took Dodo's hand, and asked, for the hundredth time, his heart bright and staunch with pride, his face luminous with the spotless sweetness of the very young and very loved, "Pa did a great thing, didn't he, Dodo? That's why he got the medal. The bravest of the brave, isn't he?"

Dodo was silent.

"When the war finishes, Dodo, when Pa comes home, we'll start riding here again, won't we?"

"Wolfie, march," Dodo ordered testily.

"You look silly in a skirt, Dorothy."

This was currently Wolfie's favored riposte to an unwelcome instruction, guaranteed to annoy. Dodo scowled at the hateful name, at the hateful pleated skirt.

"And *you* have a silly name. Wolfgang is a German name."

Wolfie took no notice.

"He will be grey . . . with a dark mane . . . my horse will—"

"Quick march," Dodo instructed her one-man troop. Wolfie's world was filled with brigades and beating drums, banners and bugles. Only cavalry instructions would get the result that Dodo wanted. Wolfie gathered a set of imaginary reins, extended an imaginary lance, and galloped away, whispering to himself, "He will be brave and he will have a silver tip to his tail . . ."

Wolfie galloped all the way to the bus stop at Lancaster Gate. At the poster of the child and gas mask, his gallop faltered. Dodo waited, smiling.

"*Take care of your gas mask,*" she chanted, dangling it before him as he turned, "*and your gas mask will take care of—*"

Wolfie snatched it and galloped on.

Stacks of dark green stretchers stood between the new brick-surface shelters at Lancaster Gate. A new sign read SHELTER THIS WAY. There was a shelter at school too, but it was like a damp brown igloo inside, with garish nasturtiums on the roof. London was in a state of perpetual preparation and precaution, something immense always on the brink of happening. Everywhere the endless warnings about gas masks, everywhere the constant instruction to leave London, to "give children a chance of greater safety and health," every day the announcement that the evacuation of children from the cities would continue. But how could you leave London when no one knew where your father was, when he might return at any minute, when you only had Spud to look after you, and she didn't seem to know any more than you did?

"We *won't* leave London, never, not till Pa comes home," Dodo whispered fiercely.

"Tens of Thousands Safely Home Already," the newspapers had said last week. Dodo shivered. There'd been so many photographs of the boats of Dunkirk, so many thousands of boats. Tens of thousands of returning men, the newspapers had said, but Pa still hadn't come. There'd been no letter, no telegram, nothing.

When they reached George's corner shop, Wolfie, thinking of his sweet ration, abandoned his rein and lance, and began to excavate a pocket, groping for the coin that must be there somewhere. Dodo, giving him as always her own ration slip, hustled him inside, with her studied attitude of tolerant exasperation.

George came out, waved to Dodo, then bent to chalk a message on the stand of the *Daily Mirror* to the right of the door:

PARIS SURRENDERS

Dodo's stomach lurched, her hands flew to her mouth, and she was screaming inwardly, *Where is he? Where is Pa?* Was he on his way back? Would he be back tonight? Tomorrow?

Wolfie emerged with two ounces of lurid Torpedoes in a paper bag, a violet one in his mouth, staining his lips.

"Have we won the war, Dodo?" he asked in a loud voice.

"They've taken Paris," she said quietly.

Wolfie had to decode the progress of the war only from Spud the housekeeper's grumblings and mumblings and his sister's occasional pronouncements. He frowned, digested this new clue, then dismissed it as not fitting with his view of the way things should go.

"Pa will get another medal, won't he, Dodo?" he said comfortably.

"Home," ordered Dodo, her heart thumping a drumbeat. *Where is he, where is he?*

She remembered the tears down Pa's face when a thin and trembly voice on the radio had announced that Britain was at war. When the National Anthem started, Pa had snapped the wireless off. Spud, roused and teary, the plate of roast beef in her hands, had said, "Think of all our men going . . ." And Pa had answered, "Spud, think of all the women in Germany saying the same thing."

Only Pa could call Mrs. Spence a name like Spud. Since Ma died, Spud had taken over the running of the house and the care of the children. She was so fond of Pa, so proud to work for him, that he could call her anything. But that evening she'd looked at Pa, shocked and perhaps a little wounded too.

Dodo marched Wolfie on. She remembered the OHMS letter recalling Pa to the Army, Pa's grief and his reluctance to leave the work he'd been doing, his papers and speeches about the conditions of the coal miners. He'd wanted, really wanted to continue that work. Then the second OHMS letter had come, warning Pa to report. Dodo remembered Spud saying darkly that Pa must either report or be arrested. In the end Pa *had* gone. Dodo turned into Addison Avenue. But now Paris had fallen; Pa must be coming back from France.

"Halt," she said as Wolfie reached the iron gate of Number 25, but her troop mutinied on the generous stone steps, was launching itself at the double door, erupting through it, scattering satchel and mask across the black-and-white-checkered floor.

Spud was standing on a chair in the dining room, her sturdy figure loosely enveloped in swathes of black sateen. "Ha," she said, fitting the last hook, hands on her cumbersome hips. "Not a chink of light will escape now." Dodo hovered beside her, a question on her lips but Spud dismounted, turned from her, and said, "Wolfgang Revel, must you always be such an explosion?" She gathered up his coat, cap, satchel, and mask. Wolfie ran to the map pinned above the sideboard.

"Where? *Where?*" he asked, his small hand hovering over Luxembourg and Belgium. "*Where* do I move our men?" Wolfie's confidence in victory had survived, undaunted, the flood of black pinheads into Poland, Norway, Luxembourg, Belgium, and the Netherlands. "Better off on our own," Spud had sniffed at the fall of Belgium, happy at such concrete evidence of the feebleness of foreigners.

"*Where?*" Wolfie asked again.

Spud put her finger on the French coast. "Twenty-one miles of water is all that separates us from the enemy. Just a bit of water and it's not just our soldiers that are coming back across that water, it's the war, coming here"—she jabbed a plump forefinger on Dover—"right back here." Spud favored a gaudy and sensational turn of phrase, was prone to speaking in headlines.

"But have we won?" Wolfie asked, bewildered.

Spud shook her head.

"Then why're the soldiers coming back?"

Dodo, still hovering close to Spud, waiting for the right minute, asked finally, "Is it true? Are they—is Pa—will he . . . ?"

Spud pursed her lips and busied herself at the tea table with the plate of boiled beef. Dodo waited as Spud lamented the dangers of London, the closeness of the war, the suitability of countryside in general for children, digressing into her perpetual lament about the difficulty of knowing how to go about things when she never heard anything, when for all she knew anything could have happened and was she expected to go on forever alone?

Spud liked the children to remain aware at all times of the trying circumstances in which she had to operate. These were all familiar themes to Wolfie so he took no notice, but Dodo watched her closely.

Spud removed the remains of beef and served pudding. Wolfie stared at his bowl.

"Roly-poly with no jam is no fun."

He moved aside his bowl and emptied an old Highland shortbread tin onto the table. Lead cavalry figures spilt onto the mahogany surface.

"Will you play, Dodo?"

He picked up the horse he called Captain, after Pa's horse, and placed him upright, glancing as he did so at the photograph on the mantel of Pa on Captain, Captain's grey coat lustrous as a star against the dark crowds, the bronze cross on Pa's chest. Pa's medal for the Moreuil Wood, for the last great cavalry charge, was a flame to Wolfie, a flame to warm him, Pa's honor a light to live by.

Dodo glanced at Wolfie before turning to Spud and whispering, "Wasn't Pa on a boat—?"

Spud folded her arms. "I hear the Jameson twins have left town. And Posy Cayzer's going to an aunt in Wiltshire . . . the country's the sensible place for children." Spud looked emphatically at Ma's oil painting above the dresser, her largest canvas, of the russet and umber hills where she'd holidayed as a child.

"Are all our men coming home?" Dodo persisted. "Haven't you heard anything—?"

"Bath time," said Spud.

"It's not bath time," said Wolfie, looking suspicious because it was always suddenly bath time at awkward moments.

"How am I to know . . . ?" muttered Spud, collecting a basket of fresh towels from the laundry.